to break a vow

A Younger Man, Older Woman Romance

Violet Haze

Stoked Publishing House

To Break A Vow: A Younger Man, Older Woman Romance ©2015, 2019 by Violet Haze
*Previously titled **A Woman's Affair***

All rights reserved. Except as permitted under U.S. Copyright Act of 1976, no part of this book may be reproduced in any form, except for the inclusion of brief quotations in a review or article, without written permission from the author. Please do not participate in or encourage piracy of copyrighted materials in violation of the author's rights.

This is a work of fiction. Names, characters, places, and incidents are the product of the author's imagination or are used fictitiously. Any resemblance to actual persons, living or dead, events, or locales is entirely coincidental.

Front Cover Design by Bookcoverzone
Stoked Publishing House
Print Edition: April 2024
ISBN-13: 978-1-7355302-1-5

prologue

EVERYONE SAYS I'm a woman who has it all.

Mason, my hardworking and loving husband, who will do — and has done — anything for me since the moment we met in our sophomore year of college.

Dean, age ten, and Jenna, age thirteen; my two beautiful, smart, and amazing children who are my pride and joy.

I live in a beautiful neighborhood, in a suburb outside an ever-flourishing city, in a gorgeous house my husband had designed and built just for our family.

My family and I want for nothing.

For years now, it's been this way. My life is peaceful, secure, and never-changing much in the grand scheme of things. Sometimes, I feel as if I'm missing out on something, but then remember the grass is hardly ever greener on the other side, as they say. It's enough to ensure I stay happy with what I have.

Until, one day, it all changes.

I meet *him*.

Cole Vaughn.

At twenty-five, he's ten years younger than me, but none of that matters to him.

I'm his ultimate goal, and his prize. Chase, conquer, and keep is his plan.

I wish I could say I make it clear I'm not interested, that I tell him no and make sure we never see each other again.

I wish I could say I made him chase me at all.

But it doesn't happen that way.

Not in the slightest.

In the end, there is no resistance, only passion, and I'm sure I'll end up paying for it.

Only nothing is as simple as it seems, and my fragile shell of a life is about to explode, exposing everything for what it is, and everyone for who they truly are.

Even me.

dedication

To every person who wonders if they made the right hard choice…
The answer is, quite simply, yes.

1

"MOM, WE'RE GONNA BE LATE!" Jenna yells up at me from the bottom of the steps, her voice filled with an impatience that makes me feel like I'm the child in our relationship. "I can't be late again or I'll get a detention!"

"Well!" Hollering back at her, my words are a mixture of amusement and exasperation. "Why change your habits now? Maybe a detention is just what you need so you'll quit sleeping in."

"You're my mom, it's your job to get me up and to school on time!"

"You're almost fourteen, Jenna."

My response results in the sound of her stomping off in a huff before I can remind her that even her counselor even said she needed to have more responsibility for herself and her education.

After all, nobody would hold her hand forever, something I know too well.

Shaking my head, I finish getting ready for the day. My shoulder-length hair, which is curly and light brown, is a pain to put into a semblance of decency every morning. Today, I just decide to brush it and leave it hanging, then move to putting on my eyeliner, which really makes my dark blue eyes pop, followed by the signature red lipstick I've worn since the day I turned seventeen.

Mason adores when I do my make-up every day. Oh, he'll tell me how much he loves me whether I wear it or not, but I know the truth. He thinks I'm more beautiful when I'm done up, and because he's worked and continues to work hard so I may be at home for our children if they need me at any time, I aim to please always.

With a final glance in the mirror, I smile at my reflection, making sure to keep it on my face as I exit the bathroom, and head down the steps before entering the kitchen. Dean's scarfing down a bowl of cereal while Jenna sits at the kitchen table with her phone in hand, looking up to glare at me as I walk past her.

Mason, on the other hand, is standing against the counter drinking his coffee while reading the paper, and grins as I approach him.

"Gorgeous, as always." His compliment is followed up with a kiss on my cheek, something he does every morning once I'm standing before him. His hazel eyes twinkle as if he hasn't a care in the world, which I suppose he doesn't. "Long day today?"

"Yes."

I walk over to the fridge to open it up and pull out a bottle of water along with an apple. Looking back at Mason, I watch as his eyes darken upon me biting into the apple, and shut the fridge door with my shoulder.

Swallowing the bite, I lick my lips in a tease before beaming at him while reiterating what my schedule is for the day. "I have to go dress shopping for April's wedding which is next month, help the ladies at the club with a few upcoming fundraisers, and I was informed yesterday I have to go have a chat with Jenna's math teacher because she's failing already and it's only two weeks into the school year."

"I hate math." Jenna mutters this as Mason's gaze leaves mine and locks on our daughter. "And the teacher's an asshole."

"Jenna—"

Mason cuts in, standing up straight as he sets his empty mug on the counter, and takes an assertive step toward her. "You will not curse in this house, young lady, or you'll find yourself grounded with nothing to do except stare at your wall for a long while."

Jenna, in her usual manipulative fashion, stands up with watery eyes and wobbly lips, screaming as she stalks out of the kitchen. "I hate you! I hate all of you!"

Before Mason can go after her, as I know he wants to, I grab his arm and shake my head with a soft smile when he looks back at me. "Just let her go. It's a teenage thing, and I was told if they don't hate us, we're not doing our job right."

"Right." He snickers, leaning down to capture my

lips in a soft, sweet kiss before releasing me with another grin. "My parents used to say the same thing."

"They were smart. After all, they told you marrying me was the smartest decision you ever made, remember?"

"Yes, and they were right." He laughs as his words, along with his suggestive wink, make me blush, and shoves a hand through his shortly cropped brown hair while looking down at his watch. "All right, I've got to get to the office. It'll be another late night, I believe."

He sets the paper down on the center island, pecks my lips once more, and says, "Love you," before walking off.

I don't get a chance to say it back as he strides out the back door not even a few seconds later. He rarely ever hears the words from me because he's always off before I can reply, but he doesn't seem to care one way or the other. We both know I'm not going anywhere, not when he gives me everything I can possibly want or need.

Dean is finishing up his cereal, slurping the milk obnoxiously as I take another bite of my apple and grab my purse. Shoving the not yet opened bottled water inside it, I call out to my daughter. "Let's go Jenna. Time to leave."

My son jumps off his stool, puts the bowl in the sink, and runs around me to quickly put on his shoes, then grabs his book-bag as I pull out my keys and stand by the back door. Dean's the first out the door while Jenna drags her feet with a glum look on her face as she follows a minute later.

I refrain from saying anything to her as I lock up the house and get into the car.

The high school is only about ten minutes away by car, and when I pull up in front after an amazingly silent commute as neither of my children said a thing the whole way, Jenna turns to look at me with a frown. "I don't want to go. Don't make me."

"Don't be absurd." It's hard to keep the annoyance out of my voice, since she says this every morning, and I'm getting real tired of it. "You have to go, you know you do, so stop whining and get going."

She stares at me for another moment, biting her lip in a way that looks so painful I want to ask her to stop, and finally drops her tear-filled gaze from mine as she grabs her book-bag from the floorboard. "Fine."

"I'll pick you up after the meeting with your math teacher. Be sitting out front and don't try anything funny."

"Yes, ma'am." Her statement is sarcastic as she opens the door, steps out, and makes sure to slam it shut before heading toward the building.

I don't know what her problem is, as always, which makes me want to start cursing in frustration. I won't, of course, since Dean is in the car, but I'm saddened a few minutes later when he finally speaks as we drive to the middle school.

"She's been so mean for the last year, Mom. She was always so nice. Why is she so mean now?"

"I don't know, honey. I wish I did."

"Me too." He doesn't say anything else, so neither do I, and when we pull up to the school he says, "Hey, Mom?"

"Yes?"

"Even if Jenna hates you, I don't. I love you."

With a soft laugh, I place the car in park at the curb, and turn to look at him. "She doesn't hate me, she's just mad at the world I guess. And I know. I love you too, sweetie. Now go have a good day."

In his usual fashion, he exclaims while opening the door and climbing out, "I will!"

A moment later, he's gone and I'm driving off, my thoughts instantly moving to everything I have to do today.

And for the majority of it, the day is like every other one has been in my life.

Until one moment changes everything.

2

MY HEELS TAP-TAP against the floor of the hallway as I head to my daughter's math classroom, where the teacher said he would be waiting for me. School's just let out, and I didn't see Jenna on my way in, yet I've no doubt she'll be waiting for me outside like I told her to. She might be mouthy and a big brat lately, but she's never disobeyed her father and me in such a direct way. She wouldn't dare.

As I enter the room, a man about my age stands up with a smile, and holds out his hand as I approach.

"Thanks for coming in, Missus Wright," he says as I slip my hand into his, which he shakes firmly before dropping, and sits down while smoothing his tie. He nods at the seat across from the desk. "I'm Mister Graham. Please, have a seat."

I do, and while he starts talking about Jenna's complete lack of cooperation in class, I study this man my daughter calls 'an asshole' and wonder what she's talking about the more he speaks. He comes across as smart, is direct, and has excellent manners.

When he pauses after explaining Jenna hasn't turned in any homework in his class since school began, I can't help but frown. "I'm sorry. Jenna's been having a lot issues for a while now. We've gotten her into counseling, but she just seems to be getting worse, and doesn't even want to come to school."

"I taught Jenna in middle school, and she was such a bright student in sixth grade, really excelling when I tutored her as well. But now…" He sounds almost as sad as I feel about this whole thing, which makes me truly wonder what the hell my daughter is thinking. "I moved up to teach ninth grade this year, which is what I wanted to teach originally, because a spot opened up. It's sad to see one of my best students failing so miserably."

I nod in agreement with him. "She's struggled ever since about halfway through seventh grade. We got her more tutoring last year and such, it helped for a while."

"I appreciate you coming in, Mrs. Wright. I will continue to keep you updated about Jenna's performance in this class. I've got some papers here…"

For the next fifteen minutes, he shows me various options for helping Jenna with her studies, many of which we've already tried. I mostly worry about having a conversation with Mason about what to do with our daughter who apparently has given up on school completely from the sounds of it.

I promise the teacher I will check in with him as well if anything comes up, and I pull out my phone while leaving the room to text Jenna, letting her know I'll be outside in a few minutes.

And just as I'm pressing the send button of the text, I walk straight into a hot and extremely hard wall of male body.

The force has my heel slipping on the floor and strong arms wrap around me just before I hit the floor, although it doesn't prevent my phone from flying out of my hand, making me wince as I hear it clatter and break apart when it meets the tile.

"Whoa. I didn't see you there."

His voice is rich and deep — you know the kind where it's incredibly sexy now but if it went much deeper it would be scary — and my body responds instantly with an arousal unlike any I've ever experienced. Caught off guard, my breath is stolen before I can even take one.

I lift my head from where it rests against his chest, his strong and firm yet gentle grip on me lessening as he makes sure I'm steady on my feet, and my eyes meet his as my heels touch the ground once more.

I can't believe the masculine younger man standing before me. He's got eyes the color of jade, curly black hair pulled back into a short ponytail, an equally black goatee trimmed short, and he's tall. So tall, which is amazing since I'm five-eleven, and meeting a man who can beat me out by six inches at least, such as the man before me does, is rare.

He smiles as I stand there gawking at him, the look in his eyes knowing as he sweeps his gaze from the top of my head to my toes, before coming back up with an even wider grin on his face. "The name is Cole. And you are?"

My first name tumbles from my lips before I even think better of it, my brain short circuiting as my body reacts in a way I'm trying to ignore with every fiber of my being. "Leighton."

"A beautiful name for a lovely woman." He winks at me before walking over to the wall and picking up the pieces of my phone.

I know I should probably do something other than stare — like pick up the other pieces which are close to me — but my whole body isn't able to do anything except gape at this man who ran into me and turns me on with the mere sound of his voice. Not even Mason has ever managed such a thing when it comes to the chemistry between us.

Cole walks back over to where I'm standing once he has all the pieces, putting it back together and holding it out to me as the start up jingle plays.

"You really should get a case for that." His comment is accompanied by a soft chuckle as I take the phone from his hand and blush while sliding it into my purse. "Are you just going to continue to stare at me... Leighton?"

My name is music on his lips and much as I wish I could speak, somehow my ability to do so coherently is gone.

And I've no doubt he knows; the way his gaze keeps dropping to my lips tells me so. His desire to kiss me is written all over his face, and I wonder if we weren't in a school, if he wouldn't hesitate another second in giving in to his natural urge.

Even worse, if he did… would I let him without protest?

"I'm just leaving for the day." He holds his arm out for me to take as he offers, "Would you like me to walk you out as well?"

As my phone buzzes loudly in my purse, I find my voice, and give a small shake of my head. "Ah, I think I've got it."

"All right." He drops his arm like it's no big deal — it's not, I have to remind myself — and slides his hands into his jean pockets. "You look familiar. Have we met before?"

"No, but my daughter Jenna Wright and I look a lot alike I'm told. You probably know her—"

His eyes round, darting down to take in my svelte form and back up again before the wicked gleam in his eyes returns as he gives out a low whistle. "I do and I see the resemblance, but you can't be Jenna Wright's mother. You don't look a day over twenty-five."

I can't help laughing at his blatant flirting. "Add ten years to that, buddy, but I appreciate the compliment all the same."

"No shit," he blurts out, his eyes getting more round than I would think is possible, and he just stares at me as if he doesn't believe I'm possibly that age. I could ask his age, but I'm sure it'll be easier to find in the school directory online, and less embarrassing than me asking as if I'm interested.

I am. Well, my body is, but my brain knows better.

Ugh. I shove the whole thing to the side and clutch my purse closer to my side, keeping both my hands occupied to keep them out of potential trouble.

With another laugh, I point down the hallway. "Well, I've really got to get going. Jenna's waiting for me outside. It was nice to meet you."

As I start to walk away, he falls into step beside me, his voice filled with amusement as he tells me, "Like I said, I'm leaving as well. And by the way, I am the PE teacher and baseball coach."

"That explains why you look like you could pick me up and break me in half — you spend your whole life exercising."

"Not all of it," he teases as we reach the main hallway, the doors to the exit outside rapidly approaching. "Do you work out?"

"Sometimes, when I'm bored." I snicker at the sound of his slight choking sound of laughter beside me, and decide to clarify my statement. "I mean, I will do the treadmill, run a little, but really I don't like working out like that in general."

"Well," he says in a low voice, placing his hand over mine as I go to open the door so I can't and leaning in close to my ear before he continues in a hushed tone. "Whatever you're doing, keep it up. Your body is smokin', Leighton."

I should tell him to stop, to back off, to not talk to me that way.

But, this younger man is looking at me as if he wants to eat me up, and a big part of me wants to let him. It's the part that wishes for a life with more excitement and less of the same stuff day in and day out; the things my husband can't give me because he's just who he is and I'm me.

I don't reprimand Cole. I don't give him a dirty look.

Instead, I gently slip my hand from underneath his, smile nice and wide until he's wearing an equal expression, and then I dip around him to another door, slipping out and away before he can say anything else.

Jenna is waiting outside as she should be, and is so silent on the way home, I have time to contemplate what the hell just happened. Mostly, its left me thinking if I hadn't run into him before now, the chances of running into him again unless I visit the school is slim, so I can easily avoid the temptation to give in to the blatant invitation in his gaze.

We quickly arrive home after picking up Dean, who darts from the car as fast as he can, while Jenna fails to notice the car has stopped moving since she's lost in her own world.

She jumps when I touch her arm, jerking her head to look at me with a glare as she snaps, "What?"

I'm so sick of her attitude, but mostly just tired, and a heavy sigh escapes despite my efforts to appear unaffected. "You're welcome to stay in the car all evening, but if you hadn't noticed, we're home now."

Without waiting for a response, I grab my purse while opening my door with my left hand, and get out, slamming the door behind me with childish satisfaction before heading inside.

Jenna follows minutes later, heading straight upstairs to her room just as her brother has, leaving me with nothing to do except make dinner a few hours from now. So, I head to my room which has its own little office area connected to it, and relax while reading a book, hoping it will take my mind off all my worries for once.

But it doesn't. Nothing ever does.

And now the attraction I felt to Cole is another thing added to the pile, mostly because it reminds me of how long it has been since Mason and I even fooled around, let alone had sex. Our sex life had been great up until I gave birth to Dean, and after that, it slowly dwindled down to nothing as of three years ago. Wasn't for my lack of trying either; Mason would just give me a kiss and say, 'not now' until I gave up attempting to start anything.

I long ago assumed he was having an affair, but he never gave me a reason to think so, nor have I ever found any proof. Either way, it doesn't matter; as I remind myself every time something makes me think about leaving, we both know I'm not going anywhere. I promised him I'm his forever, and he'll always make me keep my promise.

For a brief second though, I wonder what it would be like to have Cole give into the desire I saw in his eyes, and whether or not it would be worth the consequences.

The fact I can't answer that with a definitive yes or no means I need to avoid Cole as much as possible.

I just sure hope the universe listens.

Yeah…it doesn't.

3

BARELY A WHOLE DAY passes before I run into Cole again.

I've been out riding my bicycle for a good hour. It's one of the few activities I enjoy outside, so when the weather is nicer and I won't freeze because of getting lost in how much I enjoy cycling, I ride around for a good bit. This time of year is best though; the weather is still warm but not overly hot, so that's when I do it the most.

Just like every other time I go out, my turning around point is at a park with a lake in the center, which is where I rest a little before heading home. I'm riding down the path to lock my bike up before walking down to the sandy beach area when I see Cole jogging past me.

Well, we spot each other at the same time.

He stops running but still jogs in place, and I bring my bike to a halt, looking over my shoulder as he jogs back until we're side-by-side. His eyes immediately fall to ogle my legs, bared due to the fact I'm wearing shorts, but they don't stay there long. He pulls the buds from his ears and raises his eyes to meet mine.

"What a nice surprise, Leighton."

I don't miss the way his gaze is filled with heat, his desire blatant, and my body responds of its own accord. My nipples go taut underneath my tank, and when I squeeze my legs together in an attempt to ward off the rush of pleasure, the growing smirk on his face lets me know he's completely aware of my unwanted visceral reaction to him.

"Cole." I acknowledge his greeting with a nod, then look toward the lake for a moment before meeting his gaze once more. "First time I've seen you here as I come here rather often. Are you stalking me already?"

He chuckles, shaking his head, and lifts a hand to rest mid-thigh on my leg. The scorching heat of his hand sends a zing of awareness through me, and I suck in a sharp breath at his touch as he steps closer. He's tall enough we're face-to-face with me sitting on the seat, and his movement traps one leg between him and the bike, making me unable to escape even if I wanted to.

I have to admit there isn't one part of me that doesn't.

As we stand there, I'm not sure what I expect even though I know he wants me, but what's unexpected is him inclining his head until our mouths nearly brush and whispering, "Come have a drink with me."

Caught off guard, I hesitate in answering, but he

must take it as me not wanting to say yes because he presses his lips to the corner of mine, soft and firm. "Just one. I live right around the corner. We'll be all alone there."

All I think as he sits there with his hands and mouth on me is 'and there it is.'

This is my invitation to sin; a proposition which would be foolish to accept.

And one I have no true desire to say no to, but I won't make it easy for him. Not when one wrong move will screw everything up.

"What makes you think I wish to have a drink or be alone with you?" I place my hand over where his rests on my thigh, my fingers curling around his palm to keep his hand from moving, and draw my head away until I'm staring him straight in the eyes. "You know I'm married, don't you?"

"Yes." Bringing his free hand up to my face, he uses the pad of his thumb to stroke my cheek, his face growing serious now as he asks in a low voice, "How long have you been lonely? How long since you've been touched? Loved?"

Even as I blink in surprise at his acute perception, a deep gladness takes root, because it's been so long since anyone's known how I really feel on the inside without me telling them. I can't even remember the last time someone asked me how I was doing, with pure honesty and desire to hear my answer. "How do you—?"

He cuts me off, the same thumb which seconds ago stroked my cheek covering my mouth, and then shakes his head. "It's written all over that gorgeous face of yours. In the way my mere touch sends your heart racing." A slight move of his hand south gives credence to his words, the pulse in my throat matching the jump of my heart, which brings a naughty smirk to his face as his request turns into a demand. "Follow me back to my place and let me touch you the way you like."

It's impossible not to balk at the blatant temptation even as my skin heats up at the visions which dance through my head at his words. "I—I shouldn't. I need to be back by…I need to make dinner."

His face softens as I stumble over my words, and he hushes me again with a single quirk of his brow. "How long do you have?"

"Ah…" Swallowing, my eyes flutter shut as I tamp down my anxiety, and take a risk for the first time in nine years. "I need to be back in an hour. No later."

And just like that, he's gone from my space, waiting until I open my eyes to speak. "Done. I'll start to run. You follow." He rattles off his address. "You'll go to the back door, it's down a small alley. Coming in that way will protect you, all right?"

The fact he acknowledges my need for this to remain a private thing makes me like him more, and once I nod, he takes off running after winking at me.

Am I really going to do this? Engage intimately with someone I don't know that well, while married and understanding what all that might lead to?

The answer is yes, *hell* yes, because he's a gorgeous

man, and I'm a woman who has gone without for too long.

So, with a deep breath in and out to gather my courage, I allow temptation to lead me astray, biking straight to Cole's place.

Before long, I'm entering his place, he's locking the door behind me and grabbing my hand, taking us into the living room. Under normal circumstances, I might take in my surroundings, but in this moment my focus is all on him and nothing else.

As he goes to walk off once I've taken a seat on the black leather couch, I clasp his hand tighter to prevent him from leaving, and he lets out a small, deep chuckle. "You want that drink or no?"

"It's better if I don't." I speak softly, as if afraid we're going to get caught even while inside the protection of his place, and tug on his hand again, this time getting him to sit beside me as I want him to. Need him to. "Drinking and cycling don't mix."

He squeezes my hand in understanding even as his lips curve in amusement, and after a small moment of what I would consider awkward silence — at least on my end — he says, "My bedroom will be more comfortable for both of us."

In a moment of anxiety, now that the decision is right before me, I question him in a hushed voice. "Do you know what you're doing here? Have you ever…?"

"Yes, I realize I'm playing with fire, and I don't care. I've no doubt you're worth it." He rises again, his grip on my hand pulling me along with him until I'm on my feet, and he leads the way to the bedroom. "And no, I've never done anything like this before."

I should say I'm not looking to change my situation, make it crystal clear to him that this can never be anything serious even though I have no idea what he wants other than to fuck me right now. And that's what I want as well.

Still, he deserves to know what messing with me might mean, and he should hear it from me before this begins.

But perhaps he already knows; he has to. Where could he possibly imagine this thing between us will go with me being married?

I don't want to say anything to spoil the moment right now, so I don't, especially as we enter the room and he sweeps me into his arms before placing me gently in the center of the bed. As he slowly and tenderly removes my shorts and panties, baring me to his gaze as he places himself between my legs, I take my tank off so I'm completely naked.

I cover my eyes with my arm, telling myself it's to protect myself from the sunlight shining in the through the slightly-open blinds covering the window, and not from Cole's hot gaze as he watches me from his position.

"When's the last time you had an orgasm you didn't give yourself?"

The question has my cheeks flushing scarlet as I squeak out one simple word in reply. "Years." Way, way too many years for me to admit to out loud for sure.

"That's about to change." He laughs as my face

burns hotter, if that's even possible, before his tone takes on more of a commanding attitude. "Don't cover your eyes. Move those lovely arms of yours until they are beside you. Feel free to grab the sheets if you need to."

I do as he says, and he lets out a knowing chuckle as I fist the sheets in preparation of what I sense is coming. Well, besides me.

"That's it. Now, close your eyes and just enjoy me pleasuring you with my mouth, honey."

I feel his fingers part my labia seconds before his hot breath is so close I know his mouth isn't far behind. Then, more commands, ones I find oh so sweet even in this vulnerable position of mine, because there's no guessing, no thinking. I want to do nothing except feel right now.

"Wrap those legs around me sweetheart." As I do, he practically growls out, "God, you're luscious. Anyone who goes without fucking you for years is an idiot."

Hearing those words makes my heart squeeze with an affection for this man I've not even known a day, so different from the one I married, and barely manage to keep myself from weeping. Instead, I let out a little laugh and tell him, "No disagreement from me."

With his free hand, he cups one ass cheek, clutching it firmly as he tilts my hips up just a little and breathes in deeply.

"Oh god." I manage to squeak out the words through my massive embarrassment, feeling the heat on my face spread down my body. "I should—I should shower."

"Leighton." Tone firm, his breath is hot and heavy on me as I try to get away and fail. "Relax. I'm sure you'll taste as good as you smell. You're so aroused right now, I'm afraid if I don't get you off you're going to burst into flames."

My voice is so small, filled with anxiety even as what he said makes me want to laugh because it's true, and I hate it. "Are you sure? I've…I've never had…nobody's ever—"

His head snaps up then. "What? Are you serious? Not even your husband?"

"Y-yes." The ire in his eyes and disbelief in his voice makes me feel better even as I admit something I've never told anyone else, not even my best friend. "He said he doesn't enjoy doing it."

"But I bet you he likes receiving, huh?"

"Of course."

"Asshole," he mutters, making me smile in agreement as he moves his face back into position. "Leighton?"

"Yes?"

"This is one of my favorite things to do to a woman."

He doesn't give me a chance to reply before his mouth is all over me. The first lick is electric, setting all my nerves on edge, and so unexpected my hands clutch the sheets in my fist with an almost painful intensity. His tongue moves, his pace speeding up after that, and I am completely lost in every single delicious sensation, my body coiling higher and higher toward the orgasm he's promised me.

He flicks my clit with his tongue, over and over, inserting one finger and then two inside me. They curl up, stroking me as his tongue teases me on the outside, until he sucks my clit and thrusts his fingers hard, making my body shake as I come with an intensity I've never experienced before.

The orgasm is so powerful it sends the emotional impact of what I've just done into overload, and I can't stop the deluge of tears as I start sobbing while the aftershocks of the orgasm spreads through my body.

Cole must've expected it though, because suddenly he's lying beside me, rolling me over until I'm cradled in his arms with my head against his chest. He kisses the top of my head, his hand stroking down my hair as I continue crying, and the sweetness only makes the tears fall harder.

"That's right." His words are soothing while he hugs me tighter. "Let it all out."

My words are stuttered when I manage to speak. "Let out what?"

"Your pain, and your loneliness." He continues after another kiss atop my head. "And your fear. Everything will be okay."

I don't know why he's trying to reassure me, but I reply through my sniffles anyway, the tears slowing down to a trickle. "I know."

"No, you don't." Slowly, he draws away and sits on

the edge of the bed, looking back over his shoulder at me with a brilliant smile. "But you will. I promise."

He stands up and holds out a hand to me. When I give him a confused look, he laughs. "Come on. Let's get you washed off so you can get going in a bit."

For a moment, with the way he's looking at me, and what he's just said, I feel as if he *knows*. How, I don't know, but it's like he can see it all, and he's got it all figured out. But that's impossible, because nobody knows, and there's no way to find out.

So I brush aside the thoughts, enjoying this little time I have with him, and place my hand in his.

And it's only on my way home a little while later that I realize at no point in the brief time we spent together had he made it about anything except me.

It's the lone thing which makes me decide there's no way I will not see him again because anyone who would put me before themselves for the first time in my life is someone worth keeping around.

4

A WEEK LATER, I'm sitting in the living room when Dean comes in, practically brimming with excitement with an eager look on his face.

"Mom, can we go to the fair?"

I almost ask what fair when it clicks and set my book down on table. "Oh. That's this week, isn't it? It completely slipped my mind."

"Yah. Can we go?"

"Of course we can honey." I pick up my phone from the table and swipe the screen. "Let me just text your father and let him know where we're going so he doesn't worry."

"Yes!" He jumps with both arms in the air, and when he lands, whirls around after saying, "I"ll go tell Jenna we're gonna go."

"Tell her we'll leave in ten minutes," I yell after him while opening up a text to send to Mason.

"Going to the fair with the kids. Forgot all about it until Dean

reminded me. They close at eleven."

I don't even get a chance to set my phone down before he responds, which is unusual, and I open it up to see a short response.

"Be back by nine."

I want to say all sorts of things, like how it's Saturday, already three in the afternoon, and eleven isn't that late. Or how it's the day before the last one for the fair and it's gonna cost good money. Maybe how we'll be home when it's over and not a minute before because dammit, the kids want to have fun.

But I don't, because it's pointless to argue with him; if he wants us home by nine, we will be, and the kids and I sure as hell won't like it. I take a long and deep breath, calming down my irritation and shoving it aside for the agreeable wife I am before replying with what I know is an acceptable response.

"We'll see you then."

He doesn't respond after that.

Typical.

By the time I get ready, the kids are bounding down the steps, and it's Jenna's smile which sticks out the most. It's the first time I've seen her do anything besides frown in a while and I'm instantly glad we're doing something that makes her happier.

"Let's go. Your father wants us home by nine, so every minute counts."

They both look sad at that announcement, but neither say anything as they walk past me and out to the car as I lock up behind me. Why would they? Both know their father makes the rules and we all follow them, even if we don't like them. Well, not that I would tell them I disagree; if there is anything Mason and I agree on, it's that disharmony between us in front of the children is a no-no.

Pushing aside thoughts of Mason and his need to control everything, even his family when he isn't around, I make the relatively quick fifteen minute drive to the fair. Of course, finding a parking spot near the downtown area, especially with so many streets cut off for the fair itself, is no easy feat.

I manage to find a spot on my third trip around the area thanks to another car pulling out, and once parked we all hop out ready to have fun. After we're through the gate and we have our unlimited rides wristbands, the kids hug me and off they go to enjoy the fun. I know I don't need to worry about them, as both kids told me on the way their friends were going to meet them, and my kids are good kids who know what they can and can't do.

However, since I'm not quite up for getting on rides immediately, I walk around looking for some shade because of the heat.

Finally locating a bench that isn't occupied by anyone else and sheltered by a tree, I take a seat and watch all the people walking by as I pull out my water bottle and take a few drinks.

I'm also wishing I knew what Cole is up to right this moment. Is he thinking of me, too?

We haven't seen or spoken to each other since I'd gone back to his place. Not because I don't want to, but because I don't want to risk contacting him in any way I might be caught, and he hadn't been happy about the looming lack of contact. I told him my schedule, and acknowledged it doesn't leave much room for getting together, which might be good on the larger scale of things.

However, I'm sure we'll figure something out, because I want to see him again. I want him to make me feel pleasure like that over and over again. And honestly, I want to make him feel the same way — something Mason has also denied me for a long time.

But, it's not so easy, and the last thing I want for me, him, or my kids is for us to get caught.

Then, as if I've conjured him up out of the thin air, I hear his deep voice filled with happiness come out of nowhere.

"Well, if this isn't the third luckiest day of my life," Cole says when I look over at him as he takes a seat beside me, making sure to leave a little space between us for propriety's sake, and locking his gaze onto mine. "It's about time I see you again. How are you doing?"

"Getting better by the second," I tell him with a smile as I wonder what the first and second luckiest days of his life are. "I was just thinking about you."

The instant naughty grin on his face equals the glint of desire that flares to life in his eyes. "As was I, and then to come upon you, my day is made. I take it your kids are here somewhere?"

"Yes. I doubt I'll see them until time to meet at the car."

"And when is that?"

"Eight-thirty." His eyes darken, his eyes dropping to my lips, and while I want him to touch me as much as I'm sure he does, I make one thing clear. "But I can't—"

"I know." He cuts me off as he stands up and slides his hands into the pockets of his shorts. "I wouldn't dream of asking you to do anything inappropriate such as leave the kids here, okay?" When I nod, he relaxes his stance, tilting his head toward the direction he came from. "I just got done volunteering at one of the booths with my sister-in-law so I'm free now. Walk with me."

Rising, I fall into step beside him, and we head off toward the center of the fair, passing by tons of booths filled with games and food on the way there. With so many people we don't really talk, yet I enjoy just simply walking beside him, knowing he wants to spend time with me any way he can to make me happy.

As we round a corner, the crowd clears up a bit, and Cole asks, "Wanna take a ride on the Ferris wheel with me?"

"Of course."

We head that way, with him so close beside me our hands would touch if either of us would let them, and we get in line to wait. I look down at his hands pointedly as he leans against the wooden fence separating us from the ride.

"You don't have a wristband. It's expensive to pay per ride."

"Nah," he says with a wink. "I get to ride for free." He sees me lift my brow as if to ask how and laughs before answering. "I basically know every person working here, mostly because we attended school together. Otherwise, it's their parents or relatives, so nearly the same thing."

"I see."

"How about you? Are you from around here?"

"No" I shake my head and cross my arms over my chest while glancing away, thinking about home for the first time in a while. "I came for college and never left."

"It's a pretty nice place to raise a family, that's for sure." We smile at each other when I look back at him, but mine falls from my face when he asks, "Was it hard on your family when you didn't go home?"

There's so many ways to answer his question, with so many smaller details, I decide to go with the simple one. "Yes. But I got pregnant with Jenna halfway through my senior year and we got married right before graduation, so they had to get over it."

"Ah. Do you see them often?"

I shake my head. "No. Haven't seen or spoken to them in years. And no, I don't want to talk about it."

"Why not?" His lips compress into a thin line for a moment as I glare at him, and then his face softens as he says, "Sorry."

The line starts to move then as they get us onto the ride pair-by-pair, and once we're settled and locked in, Cole's hand instantly finds mine on the seat. It keeps moving as we simply sit in silence with our hands clasped until we're paused at the top while they continue to load people.

"Thank god." The phrase sounds tortured as he lifts his free hand and slides it into my hair, grasping it firmly while staring at my mouth. "I've been waiting to do this since the moment I saw you on that bench."

His mouth captures mine in a single swift and smooth motion. We only have a minute, if that, to enjoy this moment, so I throw caution to the wind and revel in our first real kiss here high up in the sky where I'm sure nobody can see us. The hand clasping mine releases only for him to slide it around my waist and pull me toward him, as close as two people can be in a ride like this, which leaves me free to wrap my own arms around his neck and then my hands into his hair.

Angling my head just the way he wants it, his tongue invades my mouth, and I moan with pleasure as every single inch of me flames to life with arousal. I'm not surprised at the way his mouth makes my body react, no doubt instinctually recalling the way he'd brought it so sweetly and swiftly to orgasm.

I never want this to end. I want him to touch me and put his mouth on me again and then have sex with me; something we both want more than anything else.

We can't, of course. And the moment the ride lurches into motion, he pulls back, making sure I'm good before completely letting go. He takes my hand in his again, both of us merely staring at one another and grinning as the ride goes round and round. That is, until he reaches into his pocket as we reach the top a final time and pulls out a thin little flip phone, holding it out to me. "This is for you. I've been hoping to run into you so I've kept it on me."

With a suggestive lifts of his lips, he leans real close and slips the phone inside my shirt until it's secured safely in one of the cups of my bra, and presses a kiss to the top of one breast before moving away once more.

Then, he speaks softly as I stare at him with wide eyes, my anxiety over getting caught with a phone no doubt clear on my face. "Text me once a day, that's all I ask. Let me know if I can reply or not, and delete the messages always when we're done talking. Do you have somewhere safe to keep it?"

"Yes." Even while saying this, I search my mind for an idea and realize the safest place to keep it is with me or close to me. Lord knows Mason doesn't touch me other than the occasional hand on my waist or a peck on the cheek and that thought alone eases my anxiety enough to smile at him. "I'll be fine."

"Good." His hand cradles my face, caressing my cheek with his thumb for a second, and then he drops it as we start to descend. "I can't wait to be alone with you again."

It's probably a good idea if he and I aren't seen together too much, but then again, it's the local fair. He's my daughter's PE teacher. It wouldn't be surprising if we were in the same place; who would think it anything other than innocent?

"Me too." I cover the hand that cradles mine with my free one before making a sweeping gesture. "But for now, we can have fun and enjoy the fair together as two people who know each other through my daughter. Right?"

He nods with a final squeeze of my hand before releasing it, clearing his throat as he agrees, the fire in his eyes dimming to a friendlier level. "Right. I'd love nothing more."

A few minutes later, we get off the Ferris wheel and head toward the next ride, and then the next. Soon, minutes turn into hours, and before I know it, it's time to head home and Cole walks me back to the car.

Of course, my kids are waiting there, and when Jenna sees Cole, her eyes grow wide even as she smiles. "Mr. Vaughn! Mom! What are you two…?"

"Just escorting your mom to the car since it's starting to get dark." His response is casual as he immediately takes his gaze off me and looks at her. "We ran into each other earlier and she kicked my butt at quite a few games."

"Oh." I swear she sounds disappointed at something but can't quite be sure as she continues talking. "I wish we didn't have to go home yet."

"Yeah, me too." Dean pipes up, rolling his eyes. "And Mom is pretty good at the fair games. She always used to beat me and Jenna at them."

Cole doesn't even look at me as he laughs, fully engaging with my children, which makes my heart squeeze a little.

"Practice makes perfect. Maybe one day you'll beat her." When Dean smiles at him, Cole reciprocates, then lifts his hand in a little wave. "I should get going.

Dean, nice to meet you. Jenna, see you at school on Monday."

He turns to me with a friendly smile. "Have a good evening."

He walks away and I have to force myself not to follow him with my gaze. It's bad enough I hated the way he said goodbye, even though I know that's just the way it is. But just because we have to be discreet doesn't mean I can't dislike certain aspects of it, especially when simply being around him makes me feel so many emotions I thought dead long ago.

I force myself to turn to my door and unlock it. "Come on you two. Time to go home."

They get in with a little bit of grumbling, but we arrive home at five 'til nine, both of them heading upstairs to get ready for bed and relax.

I go upstairs as well, creating a makeshift pouch to hide the phone Cole gave me as quietly as I can, and decide to hide it in one of my desk drawers. After putting it on silent, I tape it to the top and make sure I can open and close the drawer without anyone being able to tell something is there. Then, breathing a little easier, I grab a book and go sit in the living room, waiting for Mason to get home since he usually doesn't tell me a time to be home unless he plans to be there at that time also.

And wouldn't you know, he doesn't get home until nearly midnight after I finally give up and go to bed. I feel him slide in behind me, lying there for a few moments before getting real close and leaning over me, his breath strong with the smell of whiskey as he whispers, "Leigh? You awake?"

I know how to play this game though. It's one we've done so many times before.

"Mmm," is the sound I make, letting out a heavy sigh before rolling over while rubbing my eyes, trying to sound as confused as possible. "Mason?"

"Sorry," he mumbles instantly, kissing my cheek before rolling away so his back is facing me. "Didn't mean to wake you." Yes, he did. "Go back to sleep."

"S'ok." I want to let out a sigh of relief but I don't. Instead, I mimic his actions and turn away from him as well so he won't feel like he has to turn around and cuddle me. "Night."

His snore a moment later tells me he's out cold.

And I hate him just a little bit more than I'll ever admit to out loud.

5

THE NEXT DAY is about half over when Jenna and Dean start getting restless. Jenna wants to go hang out with her friends who are at the mall, and Dean wants to go spend the afternoon at his best friend Mark's house. So, after making sure their rooms are clean and all homework is finished, I agree to let them go, with plans to pick them both up at eight this evening.

I don't even bother asking Mason first because he took off this morning without a word, even after his little stunt last night, and I have no idea where he is or what he's doing. So, if he doesn't want to keep me in the loop like he promised he always would, then I don't feel the need to keep up on my end.

After getting dressed, I make sure to grab the phone Cole gave me and shove it inside my purse, and also my usual one, which I put in my front pants pocket before heading downstairs.

Jenna and Dean get into the car, faces bright with

happiness, and I decide even if Mason berates me later for not telling him first, seeing my kids happy is what matters most to me.

First I drop Dean off at his friends, and then Jenna and I head to the mall, which is a bit further away.

I'm so used to her not talking to me most of the time, it startles me when she says, "Mom?"

"Yes, honey?"

She smiles at me when I glance over at her, quickly turning my gaze back to the road as she asks, "What're you gonna do while we're gone? You should go do something."

"Ah, I probably should go back home, just in case your father comes back soon."

"Why?" Before I can come up with an answer that would suit, she keeps going. "You're allowed to go out too and stuff. I don't know why you don't go out more, especially because Dad's never home."

"It's okay honey, I don't—"

"No." Her voice sounds a bit as if she's going to cry as she cuts in, reaching over the center console to put her hand on my arm. "I might only be thirteen, but I'm not stupid, Mom. You've been happier in the last week than I've seen you be in a long time. Is it because of Mr. Vaughn?"

Instantly, the urge to panic takes over, my eyes wide as I look over at her. "Jenna, what are you talking about? You can't say stuff like that—"

"Mom." She interrupts me again, her eyes filling with tears, and she crosses her arms over her chest.

"Don't be mad. I won't tell Dad. I don't even like him, and he doesn't like me. He wouldn't even miss me if I died, I bet."

With my eyes back on the road, I look for a place to pull over, but we're in the dead middle of traffic and not far from the mall. I let out a heavy sigh. "That's not true, Jenna."

"He's barely around. Only time he ever says something to me or Dean is to correct us, or yell at us." She sniffles and drops her hand from my arm. "Why did he even bother having a family if he wasn't gonna be home or spend time with us anyway?"

There's probably so many other appropriate things I could tell my child right then, but I don't feel like lying about his reasons. She'll probably see through any attempt to fib anyway, so I tell her the truth as I see it.

"He spent more time with all of us when you were younger. You don't remember that, but I guess…well, I guess he's unhappy with himself and he spends most of his time at work so he doesn't have to be at home." I exit the highway, and while waiting for the light to change so I can turn, I toss her a soft smile. "It has nothing to do with you or your brother, baby. Your father loves you."

"But you guys don't love each other."

Nope. Nope, we don't — well, I surely don't love him, and I know his love is delusional — but I can't tell her that. "I love your father, Jenna."

I hate her instant reply, making it clear my daughter is more astute than I like in this situation, but it's something I am proud of in general because it will serve her well in the adult world she is hurtling toward. "Not like *in* love, mom. So, you should—"

"No." I cut her off, not even wanting her to think about such things, let alone make up fairytales in her head which could get us all in trouble if she slips up. "Your father will never want a divorce. I promised him forever, and that means neither of us loves anybody else. Got it?"

The light changes, and she nods solemnly at me with her wide, knowing eyes as I face forward and start driving again.

Once we arrive, she surprises me once more by leaning across the center, hugging me before opening her door and hopping out. Before she shuts the door, I hold up my phone.

"Call me if you need me," I remind her. "And no funny business, young lady."

"Okay." She speaks softly and as she starts to shut the door, I hear her whisper for the first time in forever, "Love you, Mom."

"I love you too, honey," I call out as the door shuts, and she smiles at me through the window before turning around and walking away.

Driving away, I wait until I've turned a corner around the side of the building before pulling into a parking spot, and take out the phone Cole gave me.

Much as I should do what I told Jenna I would do — that is, go home in case Mason arrives there — I don't want to. And yes, I'm playing with fire by not doing that, especially since I thought we had been so careful at the fair, yet somehow my daughter saw…well, whatever there is between him and I.

But how often will I get a chance to spend time like this with him? By the time I get to his place, we will have three glorious hours to be in each other's company, and I want that more than anything else. I need some time away; I need to do this for myself, even more so after the way Mason has treated me as if I'm invisible these last few years.

It's nice to be wanted, to be seen, and to be desired.

And I'm tired of worrying about the consequences of everything I do.

I open up the phone and send him a simple text. *"Are you home?"*

"Yes," comes his reply not even a minute later.

I don't even bother responding because I'm on my way to his place so fast, I'm surprised I don't get pulled over for speeding.

WHEN I ARRIVE, Cole lets me in and shuts the door behind us, his eyes sweeping me from head to toe. "How long do we have?"

"Three hours." Without pretense, my fingers find the edge of my shirt, pulling it over my head in one swift motion so I'm standing in my bra and shorts, and the shirt drops to the floor as I put my hands on my hips. "However, let's make every second count just in case, okay?"

He mimics my actions so he's shirtless as well, chuckling as he shrugs. "Who am I to argue with a woman stripping right in front of me?"

Then, he grabs my hand and drags me through his apartment until we enter his bedroom, where he lifts me into his arms. I wrap my legs around his waist and my arms around his neck as he turns around, moving until my back is against the wall, and his lips are on mine. Our mouths tangle in a messy, passionate, and slightly desperate sort of way, as if we have to have our fill because it could end abruptly any second…which is completely possible in this situation.

I move intuitively as his hands slide up my back to unhook my bra, and with only a slight bit of awkwardness of hand movements on my part, he drops the bra to the floor and cups a breast in each of his palms. His deep groan tells me he likes them, and my moan is next as he squeezes and plays with them, his thumb and forefinger pinching and teasing the nipples until they are standing at attention.

Without warning, he whirls around and carries me toward the bed after securing me in his arms, and our mouths break apart as he lies me down on it. His mouth instantly moves lower and lower, sucking and nibbling on one nipple while he continues to play with them with both hands, and I take this opportunity to grab his hair in my fists.

"So gorgeous," he mutters around the nipple in his mouth, biting it to make me cry out before chuckling as well. "You like that, hm?"

"Yes."

My answer is so softly spoken I'm not sure he hears me, but it doesn't matter, because he goes back to adoring my body and I want to cry with the way it makes me feel cherished. I can't help but compare this to how things were with Mason, who barely tolerated getting me off before climbing on top and doing this thing.

Worship my body? He would've laughed in my face had I even hinted at such a thing.

Cole moves to the other nipple, giving it the same amount of attention as the other, and before long his mouth is trailing kisses down my stomach. My eyes flutter shut, my cheeks flushing as he unbuttons my shorts, and then grabs each side before instructing, "Lift your ass up, sweetheart."

I manage to a little, which seems enough for him as he tugs them down and off my legs, his head between my legs not even a second later.

He keeps on talking, telling me what to do in a voice which brooks no argument, as if I would want to argue with him about it anyway. With a hand on each thigh, he exerts a little pressure and says, "Bend your knees so your feet are on edge of the bed, and spread those legs." I do. "Good girl."

My laugh at him calling me a girl is cut off by the gasp escaping at the wonderful sensation of finally having his mouth on me again. He licks, sucks, and teases me with his tongue and his hands to the point I'm so turned on I'm practically delirious with desire. My orgasm rises quickly and when the overwhelming sensations peak and tip my body over the edge, a cry of absolute and undeniable pleasure escapes before I can stop it.

My hands slip out of his hair onto the bed on each side of me, every inch of my body going slack with my release, as his hands leave me.

"Leighton…"

It takes me a minute to register he wants me to answer him, so I give him the reply I can manage to get out. "Hmm?"

His fingers return, spreading my labia apart for a moment before letting go again, and he leans over me to press kisses down my jaw until he reaches my ear, whispering, "Your pussy looks and tastes delicious. I would do that all day if I could."

I'm not sure what to say to that, but I'm sure my face is red when I respond. "Uh, thanks."

"Look at me," he commands while moving until I feel him hovering over my face and I open my eyes. "Good. Now say, 'I love when you lick my pussy, Cole. Please lick it again.'"

I blink at him, not used to this at all, and shake my head while staring up at his laughing eyes. "I…I don't talk that way. I've never…"

"Better late than never," he retorts with a laugh at my unfinished sentence, leaning back while bringing his hands to his belt buckle, and smiles while slowly removing it. "We'll work on it. You'll be a dirty talker just like me before long, once you realize how great it is, and how much it turns me on."

He pauses in his actions when he realizes I'm watching him and holds out a hand, helping me sit up when I take it before putting my hand on the fly of his pants. "You want to take them off? Get acquainted with my cock since it's about to become your new best friend?"

Even as I unbutton and unzip his pants, I laugh at his questions, enjoying his bluntness despite the lack of my own. "Do all the men your age talk like this?"

"Even if they do, it doesn't matter, because I'm the only one my age you're interested in fucking, right?"

I forget what I'm about to say, using both hands to tug his pants down his legs only for my eyes to round at the sight before me. He steps out and kicks them to the side, now as naked as me, and I'm still speechless.

Then, I must lick my lips because he gets close to the edge of the bed again and says, "If you want something to lick, I'm happy to say I've got something to offer right here."

My still quite wide eyes fly up to his face where he's looking down at me with a huge grin, where I manage to explain my reaction. "Your…it…it's so big. It won't fit. There's no way."

"Cock." He reaches down and takes my hand in his, lifting and wrapping my fist around him. "My cock is big and it will fit. I promise."

"I'm not sure—"

"Hey. Trust me." Removing my hand, he gets into the bed and lies in the center of it, and then holds a hand out to me. "Come on. You get on top, more control that way. Wait." As I start to move toward him, he leans across and opens the drawer of the stand next to the bed, pulling out a condom before lying back again. "You wanna put it on?"

"No." I watch in fascination as he rips the packet open, slides the condom down his length, and tosses the packet off to the side as I admit with a blush, "We never used them and once I had Dean, I got an IUD."

He grabs my hand with a smile and pulls me over to him, lifting me by the hips with little effort when I get close, until I'm on my knees straddling his lap. "This is for your protection, sweetheart. I'm clean, but I'm more than happy to make sure we don't take any unnecessary risks to keep you safe."

"I know."

I close my eyes, feeling exposed as his hand finds me and he inserts two fingers and strokes until his fingers are soaked before pulling them out, replacing them with himself hovering right at the entrance. "Tell me what you want, Leighton."

My face flames. "You know what I want."

"Say it. For me."

"I can't—"

He grabs my hips, clutching them firmly as he moves me down on him just a little until the head enters me, and then holds me there. "Tell me how much you want my cock in your pussy, sweetheart. I know you can do it."

"Please," I beg while wiggling, trying to get what I want without giving him what he wants, and failing. "Please, I…"

"Don't feel ashamed or whatever the fuck you're feeling right now, Leighton." His words are a growl and filled with an affection for me I'm not sure I deserve, let alone earned. "I love your pussy, I want to be deep inside you. Say it, sweetheart. Own it."

Turned on to the point of pain, and wanting him as much as he wants me, I push the words out even as the embarrassment expands through every part of me. "I want your…your…cock…"

My words trail off and he rewards me by lowering me a bit more, made easier by how aroused I am, but still burns a little as my body stretches to accommodate his size.

"Almost there," he says softly. "Tell me where you want my cock and it's all yours."

"In me."

Chuckling, he moves, but instead of lowering me more, he lifts me until just the tip is inside me, and I nearly sob with frustration. Which I'm sure is what he's counting on, because I curl my hands into fists and force the statement he wants to hear past my lips. "I want your cock in my…my pussy, damn you."

"Beautiful." His grip loosens, making my eyes fly up as his hands leave me, and he stares up at me with a brilliantly naughty smirk. "All yours babe, go as fast or as slow as you want."

My mouth drops open in disbelief. "That's it? Not

only do you make me say what you want to hear, you're gonna make me do all the work too?"

He leans up on his elbows, bringing our faces close together, and presses his lips against mine soft and sweetly. Then, he shakes his head while lying back down and puts his hands behind his head as he grins. "Nope. I'm letting you go at your pace, and once I'm all the way in and you're good to go with faster movements, I'm gonna flip you onto your back and fuck you hard until you're calling out my name. Any more questions?"

As I shake my head, unwilling to admit out loud Mason and I have never done this position so I'm feeling ridiculous, he grabs my hands and places them flat on his chest as he instructs, "Slow and steady."

Slamming my eyes shut, I rock back a little on instinct — and forcing myself to use the words he just made me say in my head so it's easier if he asks me again — his…cock goes a little deeper in my…pussy until it meets resistance, and I rise up again. After a few more times, he's all the way in and I gasp loudly when he starts thrusting up, immediately using my hips to match his rhythm with my movements.

The sensation of him, filling me so much I feel everything, is exquisite and torture all at once. When he adjusts me just a little, keeping me bent forward a little, and we start to move once more, something rubs me just right. I know I'm going to orgasm, and since I've never orgasmed before during sex, it's so shocking tears spring to my eyes.

"Oh god, Cole. I…oh god, I'm gonna—"

I don't even manage to get the words all the way out before it happens, and the moment my body goes slack, Cole rolls me over onto my back just like he promised.

"Fuck, you're stunning."

His compliment is lost when his mouth covers mine as I wrap my legs around his waist and my arms around his neck, his thrust inside me a second later leaving me wanting nothing except this for the next couple hours.

My whimpers and moans are lost inside his mouth, like his groans are lost inside mine each time he pulls nearly all the way out, only to slide back in with one smooth, immensely pleasurable motion. Over and over, until he thrusts one final time and drags his lips away, saying my name on a drawn out groan as he goes completely still.

His body comes down on mine, and for a few moments we rest that way, with me kissing him softly on his neck and shoulder, and him still deep and hard inside me.

Basking in how amazing it feels to be this close to someone again, I smile and whisper, "Hey, Cole?"

He turns his head and presses a kiss to my neck in reciprocation. "Hmm?"

"Just wanted to let you know you're the *only* man I'm interested in doing this with."

He chuckles, lifting his head to let me see his naughty smirk and humor-filled eyes once more as he teases me. "By it, you mean fucking, or cuddling?"

"Both."

"Good." He leans down, drawing both of us into a

long, sweet kiss, and then pulls out of me and away in one simultaneous movement. "Gotta clean up. Be right back."

He walks off when I nod, treating me to a nice view of his ass, and leaving me with my thoughts.

Doesn't take me long to acknowledge that I'm in deep, way faster than I could've imagined, and I've no desire to give Cole up. For once in a long, long time, I'm happy, and I want to stay that way.

No matter what the inevitable consequences might be.

6

"TELL ME A LITTLE ABOUT YOU," I say to Cole as we sit on his couch about twenty minutes later.

We're both still naked, and I'm cuddled into his left side. His arm is around me, my body warm even though a slightly cool breeze flows in from the open window.

It's so peaceful and quiet though, which I'm trying to soak up as much of it as I can before it's time to leave, and end up sighing because the last thing I want is to go back home and put up with Mason. Especially after he finds out me and the kids went out without me telling him first.

"First," Cole says in a light tone, kissing the top of my head. "You have to focus on being here with me. Let go of your worries, just for a little while, even though I know it's a hard thing for you to do."

"Okay."

He laughs, tightening his hold on me, and bringing his other arm around me with a sigh. "Not much about me to know that isn't common knowledge. My father died when I was two, my mother remarried when I was five, moved here with her and my stepfather. They went on to have three kids which meant I ended up with younger siblings — a brother, then two sisters. I graduated at eighteen, went off to college in the city, experienced living on campus and all that. I got lucky the PE teacher was retiring when it was time to get a job and they hired me here two years ago."

Even though he said this is common knowledge, I don't know any of it. However, I know I've been so focused all these years on just keeping myself together so Mason wouldn't fly off the handle that I no doubt missed a lot. I won't tell Cole that however; I'll just pretend I already know all that.

"Nice. But, I mean, here we are sitting naked next to each other and I don't know the important stuff. You know, like your favorite color, for example."

Chuckling, he says, "Blue. Yours?"

"Purple."

"Favorite ice cream?"

"Mint chocolate chip."

"Mmm, mine too. Pizza?"

"I'm not really a pizza lover."

His gasp of mock horror makes me laugh as he announces, "You're not human. Everybody loves pizza."

"I don't, therefore your generalization is untrue." I move out from under his arm, grinning as I sit up and look at him. "Wanna know what else I don't like?"

"Sure."

With as straight a face as I can manage, I say, "Bacon."

"What?"

The look of utter disbelief on his face is too funny, and I bust out laughing, moving to straddle his lap before he can react. Wrapping my arms around his neck, he scowls when he realizes I'm just fucking with him, and captures me in his hold with his arms around my waist.

"I'm just kidding." Cradling his face in my palms, I give his lips a soft kiss before smiling against his mouth as I tease him. "I probably love bacon more than you do, actually."

"Not possible." His eyes drop down to admire the view my sitting here like this gives him, and I feel one of his hands move from my back to my front, cupping my breast in his hand a second later as he adds in a gruff voice, "I hope you're ready for round two."

My body hums with arousal at the obvious desire in his words. "Uh, yeah. Sex twice in a day? I'm in heaven."

His left hand comes up and snatches my right one from around his neck, bringing it down and between our bodies, wrapping my palm around him with a grin. "Pretty sure you don't get hard cocks like mine in heaven, babe." When I give him a squeeze in response, his eyes close as he lets out a groan, thrusting instinctively into my hand.

Continuing to caress and tease my breast with his right hand, his left reaches between my legs and strokes me with one finger, then two. I'm still sensitive from earlier though, so when he slips a finger inside me, a hiss escapes through my teeth. He pauses his movements, opening his eyes to stare into mine.

"You okay? We can stop if you want."

"I'm fine. Just…it's been a while for me. I'm a little sore." He goes to pull his hand out with a frown and I give him a firm squeeze in protest. "No. Don't stop touching me. I want it dammit."

"Yes ma'am."

I playfully slap him on the upper arm at calling me that and he snickers, right before he wraps both of his arms around my waist again and lifts me. I can't help it, I shriek, especially as he stands and in one amazingly smooth motion, bends me over the arm of the couch.

He smacks my ass, then presses his hand on the small of my back, directing me with his words. "Don't move."

I barely resist the urge to lift my head and see what he's doing as his hand leaves me. Listening to him walk around the room, I hear him open a drawer before closing it again, and out of nowhere, smacks my ass again.

"Hey!"

When I turn my head to scowl at him, he merely stares at me with that naughty smirk on his face, and holds up his hand to show me the condom in his hand. "Like I said, time for round two. But first your pussy needs some personal attention from me."

He gets down on his knees, spreading my legs a little wider before his head is between my legs, and his mouth is delivering on his statement. All his movements are gentle though, even when his fingers join his mouth, and he slips two fingers in to stroke my g-spot. I've no doubt this is his favorite thing to do, because my body responds to his expert touch, the sensations spiraling toward an orgasm faster than I've ever been able to do to myself.

And when I come, my pussy clamping around his fingers hard, I hear him moan as I call out, "Cole!"

Vaguely registering him moving and the sound of the foil, he slides his cock inside me with one steady thrust, grabbing my hips to keep my body from going forward. This isn't like the first time though. He fucks me like he can't get enough, in and out with single thrusts that have him deep inside me every time. My hands clutch at the cushion to keep my balance, every plunge making me whimper with the mixed pleasure and tinge of pain from the sensitivity, but I don't care.

It's what I want; what I need. Because with every stroke, every groan of pleasure from him, it becomes more clear to me that I can't go on living as I have been. I want to be touched, and desired, and held. I want to matter to someone other than my children.

And it's right here, while my body shatters once more as Cole shoves himself deep one last time and stills with a groan, that I rediscover the self-love my husband had robbed me of so long ago. Something he'll never rob me of again, at least not without a fight.

What's even more amazing is when Cole pulls out, helps me up, and drags me into his arms to hold me tight, as if he knows exactly what I'm thinking and feeling.

Especially when he whispers, "You're amazing."

And for the first time in what seems like forever, I choose to believe I'm amazing, too.

COLE ISN'T happy about me leaving.

He stands next to the door, frowning as I gather my things, and when I finally stand next to him with my things, he hauls me into his arms and crushes my lips with his. Of course, I kiss him back just as passionately, not happy I have to leave now either.

I wish I didn't have to, and when he finally draws away, I know he's thinking the same thing.

"This may sound crazy…" His voice trails off as he smiles and slips one hand into his pockets, running the other through his hair. "But I'll miss you."

"It's not."

"No?"

"No."

"Good." He opens the door and stands back. "Let me know you get home safely, at least."

"Okay." As I go to walk out, I step up and kiss his cheek quickly before leaving his apartment.

It's only when I hear him shut his apartment door that I stop walking down the hallway, pull out our phone — that's how I've decided to think of it from now on —

and text him what I know he wanted to hear me say as well.

"If you think you sound crazy, then I must sound crazy… because I'll miss you too."

He replies almost instantly, as always. *"I know."*

Of course he does.

Smiling with pure happiness, I delete the messages, put the phone on silent before dropping it in my purse, and head out to my car to go pick up the kids.

I DECIDE to pick up Jenna at the mall first, sending her a message before I start driving, and she doesn't respond. Not that her failure to respond is unusual; it's not. I'm sure she'll be waiting for me as I told her to, and when I finally arrive, I'm not wrong.

Oh no. She's waiting for me, all right, but she isn't alone.

Even as I pull up to the curb and park, it's clear she doesn't see me. She isn't paying attention at all. Instead, all her focus is on the boy sitting next to her on the bench, with his hand resting on her bare knee. Her smile is bright as I've ever seen it as she stares at him, her head tossing back in a peal of laughter at something he says, with him chuckling right along with her.

I don't know this boy. To be fair, I don't know anyone she knows other than a handful of her girlfriends she hangs out with in general, mainly because Mason doesn't allow any kids to be at any house other than our own. And the only things Jenna's ever done in regard to school is after school clubs, nothing Mason nor I needed to participate in along with her.

Placing the car in park, I figure I need to watch for a few more minutes to figure out what's going on, such as whether this boy is a friend or something more. They continue talking and laughing, until finally he leans in real close and whispers something. I see the instant it becomes an intimate moment between them, his hand moving from her knee to her waist as he scoots closer, and she smiles as he moves to kiss her.

And that's when I blare on my horn.

Jenna's head rears back, her eyes going wide as she searches and finds my car where I'm blaring the horn, while the boy backs away at the same time. Shutting the car off, I step out and close the door behind me before walking over to where she now stands, and the boy rises as I approach with a nervous smile.

I don't see the point in being anything but blunt as I stare at him. "Who are you?"

He gulps, eyes darting to Jenna's before returning to mine, and he says, "Mark."

"How old are you, Mark?"

"Uh…I'm sixteen."

"I see."

Turning to look at Jenna, who has tears streaming down her cheeks and looks terrified, I point at her and then the car. "You. Go now."

"Mom—"

"Now!" She jumps like a little frightened bunny at

my raised voice — which I will feel bad for later — and tossing Mark a sad look, she runs to the car and gets inside.

Turning back to him, I ask, "Where are your parents?"

"Inside. I—"

"I don't care." I interrupt him with a wave of my hand and glare at him. "My daughter will be fourteen soon, but let's get one thing clear: she's a child. As are you. Keep your hands and your mouth off of her, because you don't want to deal with her father, you got it?"

His face blooms bright red along with his ears as he looks down at the ground. "Y-yes."

"Good. Now get out of here."

I head back to my car when he heads back inside the mall, and the moment I get in the car and shut the door, Jenna starts talking rapidly.

"You didn't have to embarrass him like that, Mom," she starts, but I lift up a hand to halt her from spewing bullshit I don't want to hear.

"*He* shouldn't have been touching you, let alone attempting to kiss you. You're thirteen, for god's sake. And really Jenna? In front of the mall where anyone could see you? Are you trying to get your ass in trouble?"

Even though her face flushes, her tone is angry as she glares at me. "No. I want to feel like a normal teenager, and I like boys. I want to hang out with them."

Starting up the car, I pull away from the curb while going right back at her. "Me letting you go to the mall to be with your friends isn't enough for you? Taking you to the fair where I let you go have fun for hours without me hovering over you isn't good enough? Now you have to kiss and let boys touch you for my efforts to count?"

"Of course not, but—"

"No, Jenna. Dammit. I know your father is strict and I try to level that out a bit by giving you guys freedom when he isn't around, but if you're just going to shove it in my damn face, I won't anymore. You can do nothing and go nowhere if you want do things you know you shouldn't. I'm highly disappointed to have seen that, because I thought you knew better—"

"I'm sorry," she wails, starting to cry, and when I look over she has her head in her hands. "I just…I just wanted to know what it felt like—"

God, I don't even want her to finish that sentence, so I cut in with a scoffing sound. "Trouble, Jenna. That's what getting involved with boys at your age feels like."

"Are you gonna tell Dad?"

"God, no. Neither of us want to deal with his reaction and you know it. Just don't do it again, or I won't be so nice next time. In addition, you do dishes all week and no going anywhere with your friends for a week."

"Yes ma'am," she whispers before falling silent and staring out the window.

I almost feel bad, but her father's grounding would be much worse, and she knows it. Any grounding is better coming from me, and since they hardly ever get in trouble, I've always been able to avoid getting Mason involved.

When we arrive home after picking up Dean, I see that Mason isn't home, which means he doesn't and won't know we went anywhere at all.

Sighing with relief, the kids go upstairs to get ready for bed, and I send Cole a message as he asked me to.

"I'm home. All is good."

His reply, when it shows up not even a minute later, makes me smile. *"Yes, you are good. Tasty too. And I'm glad. Night."*

"Night."

Deleting the messages, I put the phone in it's hiding place, dress for bed, and take a book downstairs to read while I wait for Mason to arrive home as always.

And again, I end up going to bed alone.

Only this time, for the first time in our marriage, he doesn't come home at all.

7

AFTER WAKING up to discover Mason hadn't come home at all, I find a message waiting from him on my phone.

"Worked late at office. Stayed with a friend. Home at six tonight. Have dinner ready."

What the fuck?

My first reaction is to laugh. Stayed with a friend, my ass, because if there is anything I know with certainty, it's that Mason doesn't have any friends. He's an asshole and that's a well-known fact. Nobody would be dumb enough to say it to his face of course, but I've received more 'you poor thing' looks when with him than I've ever known what to do with.

Climbing out of bed, I just shake my head, and wonder why he tells me to have dinner ready at six as I walk into the bathroom to get a shower. He doesn't usually eat at home anymore, and I honestly can't remember the last time he wanted it ready when he got home, but maybe that's because he's rarely ever home to eat anything except breakfast.

So, as I step under the hot water and wash my hair, I know two things for certain about what's going on.

One, he's probably sleeping with someone else, which I don't care about at all for obvious reasons.

And two, if he suddenly wants dinner ready at a certain time, it most likely means someone is coming over for dinner.

Who that person is I have no idea, because like I said, he doesn't have any friends as far as I know. Sighing, I contemplate what to make for dinner — which means I have to add shopping to my list today — and finish up showering.

After dressing, doing my hair, and putting on my makeup, I head down the hall to wake up the children, only to stop short at hearing the sound of their laughter coming from the kitchen.

And, as I walk down the steps and then into the kitchen, the lovely smell of bacon and eggs surrounds me while I gape at my children who are standing in front of the stove.

"Okay…" Chuckling, I take a seat at the center island and joke, "What did you guys do wrong?"

Jenna grabs a plate from the counter next to her, puts some food on it before turning around, placing it in front of me as she says, "Nothing, Mom. I've been practicing thanks to home economics class and wanted to show you my cooking skills. Dean just wanted to watch." Grabbing a fork out of the drawer, she hands it to me with a bright smile.

My heart melts at her making me breakfast for the first time ever. "Thank you, sweetheart. It smells delicious."

"Welcome. And of course it does, I made it."

We all laugh as they both make plates of their own and sit down to eat with me. It's only when we're all done and they're putting their dishes in the sink that they notice their father is missing.

Dean's the one to ask. "Where's Dad?"

I give them a modified version of the truth. "He's at work already. Long day for him." I see Jenna staring at me, the look on her face telling me she knows he didn't come home, and I ignore it. "Go finish getting ready for school so you guys aren't late."

"Okay." Dean runs out of the room, but Jenna doesn't follow.

Not really up for questions or explaining, I flick my gaze from her to the doorway. "Go on. And don't forget you have your math tutoring after school this afternoon."

That works to distract her from the topic of her father as she glares at me, hands on her hips as she shakes her head. "I'm not doing it. I told you I don't like that teacher."

"Mister Graham seemed perfectly reasonable to me and he wants you to succeed—"

"Whatever," she mutters before stomping off, leaving me as confused as always as to why she has such an attitude about school stuff lately.

Either way, long as she keeps it away from her father, I'll just give her a little leeway with it. She's obviously aware of the problems between her father and I, and I've no desire to pretend with her at her age. I know it's probably just as stressful for her as it is for me, even if I don't approve of how she deals with; not like I'm doing a better job of dealing myself.

But apparently I live in a house filled with people who are doing things they shouldn't to deal with stuff, so I shove the little bit of guilt I feel aside and carry on with my day.

AS I'M WAITING on my friend April to meet me for lunch, I send Cole a text, conscious of the fact this is his lunch time as well. *"Hey. How's your day going?"*

"Hey. Good. Was just about to text you about Jenna."

That message gets my full attention, making my heart race as I sit up straighter, replying immediately. *"What about her? Is something wrong?"*

"That's what I'm trying to figure out. Did you see the bruise on her upper arm? She told me it's from tripping?"

I've no knowledge of Jenna tripping this weekend, but she also went to the mall so it's possible. However, the question mark at the end gives me the feeling he doesn't think it's from that. *"No, I don't know anything about that. She might've tripped at the mall perhaps."*

"I don't think so." Frowning, I'm not sure what to say to that message, when he sends another a few moments

later that stills my heart. *"It looks like someone grabbed her, babe. Hard."*

Gulping while I search for a rational explanation — such as how she's not been anywhere except with me at home, at school, or at the mall, I ask him, *"Are you sure?"*

"She tried to hide it, didn't want to get dressed for gym class. Nothing about that screams innocent tripping incident to me. Does it to you?"

No, no it doesn't, but if someone grabbed her…who was it? And why?

I'm not one to jump to conclusions. I've got so much going on in my own life I know that sometimes there's a fake picture resting on top of the real image underneath. Assuming things based on initial information is likely to lead to false judgment, so I tend to make sure I've got as many facts as possible before moving forward. And in this case, that means I need to talk to Jenna when she gets home.

"No, and thanks. I will talk to her when I pick her up after tutoring."

"All right. Let me know if I need to kick someone's ass."

His concern and protectiveness make me wish he was close enough to hug, but because he's not, I have to settle for way less. *"You're sweet."*

"I know. Now…when will I see you again? ;) Soon?"

"Not tonight unfortunately. Maybe tomorrow during my run. :) I'll let you know."

"Look forward to it. Gotta go, class time. Bye babe."

Just as I'm about to reply, April's voice rings out as she approaches me from behind. "Leighton!"

She plops down across the table from me right after I shove the phone into my lap and fold my hands on the table top, greeting her with what I know is an overly bright smile. "Hey, April."

The waiter appears almost instantly, taking our drink and food order before leaving us alone, and April pulls out her tiny notebook from her purse. As usual, the sight of her bright pink pen with the fuzzy pink material on the end makes me laugh and her blush. She starts going over everything she's gotten done for the wedding, and everything she needs to do, and for a few brief moments, I'm a touch jealous.

I mainly feel that way because our lives are so completely different. We met in my first year of college as roomies. About five inches shorter than me, with her brown hair and brown eyes, as well as her naturally skinny frame, we couldn't be more different.

The first year we both studied and participated in so many things, but the following year, I met Mason and our lives began to differ dramatically. She met her soon-to-be husband Jacob at the job she landed right out of college, both of them wanting to focus on their careers for a while, and now they were finally getting married all these years later.

She lives a bit outside of town now in a house they bought together, so it's a rare day we can even get together for an hour because of our lives and schedules. Mason's never had a problem with my friendship with her, and for that I'm glad, because she's the only friend I have in the world.

Well, correction, I have two now counting Cole.

Either way, it's sad, but that's how it is.

"Earth to Leighton." I blink as April slaps the table in front of me, smiling when I meet her eyes with a blush. "There you are. I know all this stuff is kinda boring anyway. Did you get your dress?"

"Yep, I did. Thank you."

The waiter returns with our drinks and salads, both of us taking a few bites before April asks, "What are you doing this weekend?"

"Um, nothing that I know of so far. Why?"

"Jacob and I want everyone who will be in the wedding to come for the weekend. Sort of like a pre-wedding celebration for the wedding party." She laughs and lifts both her brows in question. "Think you can make it?"

"I'll…I'll have to ask Mason. If he's working, and the kids can't go to their friends'—"

"Right." Her smile is rueful. "You would think after you having kids for all these years, I'd know better by now."

"No worries. I'll let you know, all right?"

"Of course." She takes one more bite before shoving her plate away, picking up her notebook, and putting it in her purse. "Hate to run so soon but still have so much to do."

"Yeah, me too." Standing up, we both hug, and when we pull back, I shake my head as she tries to hand me money for lunch. "You know the rules. You drive to see me, I pay for lunch. Get out of here."

She laughs, dropping the money inside her purse as she steps back. "All right. Let me know asap and if so, I'll see you Friday!"

"Will do."

As she walks off, I sit back down to finish my food, pay the check when the waiter stops by a few minutes later, and then head to the grocery store while wondering who the mystery dinner guest will be.

8

I'M NOT able to talk to Jenna about the bruise right after her tutoring, mostly because Dean's in the car, but when we get home I ask her to follow me into the kitchen to talk while I prep dinner.

She hovers by the door, barely entering as I get out the ingredients I need and place them on the center isle, removing a knife from the drawer before looking over at her.

"Wanna tell me about the bruise on your upper arm?"

Her answer is a mumble, her eyes dropping to stare at the floor as she shuffles her feet. "Nothing to tell."

"Don't lie to me." My tone is sharp and she lifts her head, eyes wide as she stares at me. "Is someone hurting you?"

"N-no." She licks her lips when I lift a brow, her stuttering giving me a right to be doubtful, and she takes a deep breath before saying, "I mean, he didn't mean it, just grabbed me when I tried to walk away."

My spine stiffens at the mention of some boy putting their hand on my daughter in anything other than a nice, friendly way. "Who put their hands on you? Mark?"

"Gosh mom, no. Mark's nice. Just some asshole at school messing around, okay?" She straightens, huffing as if I'm the one who's being a pain in the ass, and flips her hair over her shoulder while making an 'ugh' sound. "It's not a big deal but I should've known Mr. Vaughn would say something to you."

As she twirls away and then rushes up the steps, her exit punctuated by the slamming of her bedroom door, I debate following her and demanding answers to her attitude. I know as her mother, I should always be on top of things, and let her know who the boss is, but her father is heavy handed enough.

He doesn't even need to be around to assert his authority over us; after all these years, we know what he wants and desires of us every moment. And I know we're all starting to break under the pressure of his expectations — me, especially.

With muted long-denied fury at him, and a heavy sigh of exhaustion due to everything else, I shove aside any thoughts that don't include the best way to prepare the chicken for dinner.

WHEN MASON WALKS into the dining room as I'm placing the food on the table, he isn't alone, just as I expected he wouldn't be.

Nope.

On his arm is a woman, and the only way to describe her is as 'arm candy,' instantly generating sympathy for the girl who has no idea what she's gotten herself into by being even that close to him.

Long, curly blonde hair, bright green eyes, and a white, toothy smile greet me as they stand in the doorway, her arm hooked through his left one.

She doesn't look a day over twenty, and I'm instantly disgusted with Mason without even knowing who she is to him, but I don't let it show.

"Welcome home, honey." I step back and clasp my hands in front of me, nodding at the table. "Please, have a seat and eat. I'll go let the kids know dinner is ready."

Leaving before either of them can speak, I elect to refrain from shouting and walk upstairs to tell the kids dinner is ready, mostly to give myself more time before having to join them at the table.

As both kids follow me back to the steps, my soft words come with a warning. "Your father's brought a guest. Be quiet unless a question is directed at you, and remember to ask to be excused before you leave the table upon finishing."

"Yes ma'am." Their reply is in unison as we begin walking down the steps, both continuing to stay behind me as I head toward the dining room.

Upon entering, Mason — in his usual show-off-for-guests fashion — stands up from where he's seated and walks over to the kids, enveloping them in his embrace as he panders to his audience. "Buddy. Princess. I'm sorry work keeps me so busy."

Dean stares up at his father with round eyes while Jenna looks at me and rolls her eyes, Mason releasing them after a second before returning to his chair.

Once we're all seated, Mason picks up the bowl of sliced carrots and puts some on his plate, then offers it to the woman, who takes it with a smile.

He does it again until everybody has food on their plates, and as everyone picks up their forks to begin eating, he keeps his eyes on the kids as he finally introduce his guest. "This is Wendy. She's my secretary and she's joining us for dinner because after we're done here, we are going out of a town for a week. Business trip."

On the outside, I don't move a muscle; on the inside, I'm practically dancing because him leaving means I can go out of town this weekend. The kids don't even react to his news, other than each mumbling, "Hi Wendy," before going back to eating their dinner silently.

That's pretty much all that happens until the kids are done, and after they've been excused and go back to their rooms, Mason puts down his fork and clears his throat.

"I trust everything will be fine while I'm gone, as always."

I just manage not to grit my teeth at his subtle insult,

as if I need reminding to be a good girl while he's away. "Of course. Smooth sailing."

"Good." He stares at me for another tense few seconds, and then nods, sliding back his chair and standing up. "I need to go pack a few things and get going, as the flight leaves in four hours."

As his wife, perhaps I should ask where he's going, but truth is I don't care. I'm just glad he's leaving and for a whole week, a length of time I haven't experienced away from him in a long time.

So, with an incline of my head, I acknowledge his statement, and he turns his focus on Wendy. "I'll only be five minutes or so."

And with that, he's gone.

A minute ticks by while the girl looks at me as if she hasn't a care in the world, and my smile is as nice as I can make it when I say to her, "How much do you know about the animal kingdom, Wendy?"

Her face fills with confusion as she crosses and uncrosses her leg before clearing her throat. "Uh, not much I guess. Why?"

I almost feel sorry for her, because it's clear she's in love with Mason, and I'm about to burst her bubble. Well aware of the fact she no doubt had no choice in coming with him here to the house — after all, what Mason wants, he gets — I decide to warn her off without saying it outright, knowing Mason will return any minute now.

Five minutes to him isn't technically that long, because he likes to keep you on edge, waiting for the moment he comes back so you don't forget your place with him.

"Well…" My tone is friendly as I respond with a smile. "I find animals fascinating. For example, some predators will lock their eyes on their prey, go after it, and tear it to shreds without waiting another second after they finally have it in their grip.

"Others are more malicious. They'll play nice, making their prey feel safe and secure, even loved perhaps, for a time. But then, the torture begins. They'll toy with them, playing games, occasionally returning to the sweet facade in order to make their prey think it's all in their imagination. Think of a cat and a mouse. The cat will toy with the mouse, patting at it with its paws while the mouse struggles to get away, because it knows eventually the cat will kill it."

Her eyes widened during my little speech, and when I sit forward with my hands clasped on the table top, her confusion switches to fear. Amused at her thinking I'm talking about myself being the predator, I chuckle and stand up, knowing she doesn't understand that I don't care about her fucking my husband. No, I am more concerned about her safety.

"You're young, Wendy, and beautiful. You've got your whole life ahead of you. Don't throw away a future dinner involving steak for leftover sausage, honey. Especially when the sausage isn't anything close to what you believe it to be."

And with that, I stride out of the room and into the kitchen, filling a glass with water and sipping at it until I hear Mason begin coming down the steps. Taking a deep breath, I return and reclaim my seat without looking at Wendy, Mason entering the room again not even a minute after me. He walks over to me with his duffel bag in hand, leans over to kiss me on the cheek, and then straightens before walking over to where Wendy sits.

He must not think anything is amiss, because he holds out of his hand to help her stand up, which she takes as he says, "Time to go so we don't miss our flight."

She doesn't look at me as she stands, her arm looping through his once more as she keeps her eyes on his but says to me, "It was nice to meet you, Leighton."

"You too, Wendy." The kindness in my voice is genuine, as always, because it's not her fault Mason's a snake. "Have a good trip, both of you."

As they walk toward the door, I can't be sure whether or not she took me seriously, and when he opens the door, she drops her arm so he can walk through with his bag. It's then she glances back over her shoulder at me, the smile still on her face, but I see it in that moment; the little spark of trepidation at what I've hinted about the man she's going on an extended trip with.

"Truly, dinner was lovely. Thank you."

And as she turns back around and leaves, gently closing the door behind her, I've no doubt she wasn't thanking me for dinner, but for the warning.

Hoping she takes that warning and runs with it upon their return, I wait to make sure the car pulls out of the driveway and heads away from the house before I turn on my heel and head upstairs to my bedroom.

Pulling out my phone, I dial April, who picks up on the first ring with clear excitement in her greeting. "Leighton! Tell me you're coming this weekend!"

"Yeah, I am, but wanted to ask if it's okay to bring someone with me."

"Bring—?" Her brief puzzlement is replaced by a laugh. "You mean, Mason wants to come?"

Now it's my turn to chuckle. "God, no. He's going out of town for business for a week. I'd like to bring a friend."

"Oh." She drags out the 'o' in a teasing, suggestive way. "A friend huh? Sure, Leighton, whatever it takes to get you here!"

I know she's curious, but isn't going to ask because she knows me all too well, and my amusement filters through as I respond. "I'll see you Friday then?"

"Yep. Can't wait!"

She hangs up without waiting for me to say anything else. With a shake of my head, I toss the phone on the bed and head into the other room, removing the phone from the drawer and dialing Cole's number.

When he picks up, his voice is filled with surprise. "Leighton?"

"Hey." I waste no time in telling him what I've called him for because I'm just too fucking thrilled at this sudden opportunity. "What are you doing this weekend?"

His bark of laughter at what I'm sure is my unexpected question lightens my heart, his next words setting it near to floating. "I think the correct answer is 'whatever you're doing, sweetheart.' Am I right?"

"Yep. So pack your bags because you and I are going out of town for my friend's pre-wedding celebration on Friday."

"It's a date."

"Yes, it is, and I can't wait."

The smile on his face is evident in his voice. "Me either, babe."

"I know." Although I'm grinning at the idea of spending the whole weekend with him, I let out a heavy sigh because Friday is still a bit far away. "I gotta go for now though, okay?"

"Absolutely. Bye for now."

"Bye."

With a little squeal of happiness as I hang up the phone, I leave the room to tell the children they'll get to spend some much needed time with their friends this weekend.

And all I can think as I walk down the hallway is that Friday can't come soon enough.

9

WE ARRIVE at the hotel where April's having her pre-wedding celebration, and once we've parked, I turn my head toward Cole with a nervous smile. "Ready to go in and meet my friends who have no idea who you are?"

He grabs my hand, brings it up to his mouth, and presses a kiss to the back of it with a grin. "Absolutely, babe. Do I need to be on my best behavior?"

"No." My grin matches his own as I finally relax completely. "They don't care for Mason and will be thrilled with how happy you make me."

It's the absolute truth, too, since everyone knows how Mason is for the most part.

"Good. I'm not sure I'd be able to resist from keeping you close to me the whole time anyway." With his right hand, he reaches over and opens his door, giving the one of mine he holds a squeeze before letting go for now. "Let's head inside."

He's out of the car and around to my door before

I've not done more than pull the keys from the ignition, opening the door and holding out a hand to assist me. Gladly taking it, I exit the car after grabbing my purse, and he shuts the door behind me, only to direct a pointed look at the trunk.

"Pop the locks. I'll carry the bags in."

Even as I hit the button on the car's remote, I protest while taking a step toward him. "It's okay, I can carry my own—"

"Yes, you can," he interrupts with a chuckle, pulling his bag and mine from the trunk simultaneously, dropping his to the ground to shut the lid. "But, you will not be carrying them right now because this is what a gentleman does for his lady when she's stolen him away for the weekend."

The way he says it has me snickering right along with him. "Well, how could I possibly object to that?"

Lifting his bag in his left hand while tossing mine over his right shoulder, he inclines his head toward the front entrance as he starts walking. "Let's get checked in and changed so we aren't late for dinner."

"Yes, let's." Laughing, I fall into step beside him, pressing the key to lock the doors before dropping my keys into my purse. "Especially since I'm starving."

"Good. The restaurant in this hotel has some of the best food in the entire state. You'll love it."

"You've been here before?"

"Yep, quite a few times with my family actually."

"Why?"

"On the way to the airport; on the way back," he

clarifies with a shrug. "If you're starving, and you know the food is good, who cares if it's in a hotel?"

"I don't!"

"Me neither."

Since he's carrying the bags, I open the door once we've reached it, and follow him through. Ten minutes later, we're checked in, and he enters our room behind me, dropping the bags on the floor in front of the king size bed before pulling me into his warm embrace.

"A whole forty-eight hours straight with you; I won't be happy when it's over."

"Shh." The sound is an admonishment given with a slide of my arms up his and around his neck, my heart racing with exhilaration at the unexpected time with Cole, along with the freedom from Mason's expectations. The fact it will be short-lived doesn't put a damper on my happiness at all, which is why all I can do is smile up into his downturned face. "How about you not think about that, and think about having dessert before dinner instead?"

Swooping in, he steals a hard, quick kiss, setting fire to my need for him only to deny me with a simple shake of his head as he puts distance between our mouths once again. "It's been too long, and when the time comes to have my way with you, I want hours to do so."

"Not even with a little visual temptation?" Lowering one arm, I reach between our bodies and pop the two buttons at the top of my sundress free, displaying a fair amount of cleavage to his heated gaze. "Do you honestly want to wait to put your mouth all over me, because I don't."

Groaning, he glances away from my display while his hands around my waist grasp the fabric tightly, declaring his internal conflict without a word. When he looks back at me a few seconds later with a determined expression, I fear I've lost the battle, and release an exaggerated sigh of disappointment.

But instead of letting me go, he whirls me around and follows my fall down onto the bed, his body trapping mine against the mattress as he captures my smiling lips with his hungry ones. The kisses quickly turn from sweet to deep, slow french kisses, and a happy giggle from me is lost between our mouths.

He slips his right hand down from where it's trapped beneath my waist until he's touching the bare skin near the hem of my skirt. Skimming his fingers along my thigh and underneath it, he nears the juncture of my thighs with every second that passes, yet stops short to tease me with the heat of his hand instead of touching me like I want.

Feeling more like a horny teenager wanting to have sex with her boyfriend no matter the consequences, instead of a responsible grown woman who needs to change and head downstairs for dinner, I beg for his touch with a lift of my hips. His ragged mixture of laugh and moan in my mouth encourages my hands to find a new place to rest, clutching his hair with both until he yanks his lips away with another snicker.

"Mm-mm." He admonishes me at the same time he

pushes the fabric of my underwear to the side. Slipping one finger inside my more-than-ready body, he curls a finger up to rub my g-spot and make me squirm. "Fuck you're so wet for me. I think making you wait is precisely what I'm going to do."

"No." My protest is more of a small wail and he laughs again when I try to grind against his hand, begging as my eyelids drift shut. "I've been waiting. It's been so long and…please."

"There's no chance in hell we'll make it to dinner if either of us frees my cock at this moment."

I don't even need to open my eyes to know his eyes are blazing with want, nor would discovering his cock hot and rigid and ready to go surprise me. He wants me as much as I want him, and even though my body is ravenous for him, I understand why he wishes to wait.

"I know." Letting go of his hair, I gasp as he inserts another finger. Curling it up to stroke in unison with his other digit, my lower body moves with his rhythm. "But my body doesn't care, and if you don't finish the job, I will."

"Gladly." With no warning, he gradually makes his way down my body, bending my legs before placing them over his shoulders, and begins utilizing his hot mouth and tongue in conjunction with his fingers.

Needing something to hold onto as he flicks the tip of his tongue hard and firm over my clit, I grab onto his hair again. The vibrations from his chuckling are just what I need to send me over the edge, my eyes slamming shut as I cry out. "Oh, god!"

His free hand clutches my ass, keeping my body riding his mouth as I come, and when it ends he gives me one final lick before blanketing my body with his once more. This makes his arousal evident between my legs, but when I remove my hands from his hair and start to slide one down his body, he grabs it with a shake of his head.

"Mm-mm. Dinner."

Forcing my heavy eyelids to lift, the smile I give him is a content one mixed with a little glee. "You just got me off with your mouth, and all you can think about is food?"

He grins down at me, happiness lighting up his whole face. "Babe. Either I think about food, or we won't be leaving this room until morning, and like I said, I want to take my time."

"Fine," I grumble with an exaggerated pout, but really, I love the fact he wants to take his time later.

Laughing, he hops up and holds out a hand, helping me rise as well before removing his shirt. "Join me in the shower."

"Sure that's a good idea?"

He pops the button on his jeans as he walks toward the bathroom and winks at me over his shoulder. "Of course. I need someone to wash my back."

Not waiting for a response, he walks out of my sight, and after a quick decision, I pull the sundress over my head at the sound of the shower being turned on. By the time I join him, he's already soaped up his hair and has his head tossed back while rinsing it out.

When he finishes, he reaches out to grab my hand, presumably to tug me under the water with him.

Instead, as he watches with desire flaring in his eyes, I lower myself to my knees and take his cock into my hand, giving it a squeeze while keeping my gaze locked on his.

Needless to say, once I lean in and place my mouth over the tip, he doesn't even try to stop me…and we end up walking in to dinner ten minutes late.

WHEN COLE and I step into the dining room, April wastes no time in grinning at me. As we approach she declares in a loud voice, "I'd be late to dinner, too, if I were you and had that fine specimen by my side."

Cole tugs me closer to him with an arm around my waist and a chuckle, while Jacob turns toward April with a confused frown. Upon noticing she's talking to me, though, he grins right along with her and eyes the man by my side with interest.

I've always liked Jacob; he's down to Earth and sane, which balances well with April and her quirks. Neither of them ever liked me being with Mason. And it would be a blatant lie if I said I don't enjoy the fact they take to Cole from the moment we sit down across the table from them.

Jacob grabs him up in conversation about work within minutes, which is when April stands up with a blatant look at me and announces, "I need the ladies room."

Quite mindful of the fact she wants to talk about Cole with me, I lean in and tell him in an over-loud whisper, "Be right back. She wants girl talk."

"I have sisters," he retorts with a chuckle, turning his head to press a firm, soft kiss on my lips, and setting off the suggestive hoots of everyone at the table simultaneously. "I know how it goes. Don't worry about me."

April tugs at my arm, pulling me up from the chair, and only lets go after we've entered the hallway with a single demand. "Spill it."

I adopt an innocent look as she tosses a glance my way. "Spill what?"

"Why a man who isn't your husband has his lips on yours, for starters." She pushes on the door to the ladies room and once inside, walks up the counter to stare into the mirror, catching my gaze through it with a devilish smirk. "Come on. You know I've never liked Mason, so give me the details. All of 'em."

She listens to everything from start to finish about how Cole and I ended up together, her eyes widening when I finish spewing my feelings. "Words are inadequate to describe how he makes me feel, April. I haven't felt this way in…in such a long time."

"Aw, honey." She laughs, her smile big and happy, turning toward me before enveloping me in a tight hug. "That feeling is called falling in love, and I doubt you've ever felt it for real."

"That's not true—"

"Yes, it is." Her tone is gentle, but her words are fierce she pulls back to stare into my eyes. "I've been waiting a long time to see you like this, for you to be more like the Leighton I knew in college before she met Mason than the woman who's been barely living her life for years now."

I don't know what surprises me more: the fact she knows, or that she's not said anything to me about it. "When…?"

Sliding her arms down mine before crossing them over her chest, she lifts a brow as her lips flatten. "Seventeen years, hon. That's how long we've known each other; how long we've been friends. You think I didn't notice the way he changed you? The way you changed for him?"

I see the worry now, and the hurt, both of which I never picked up on. Sure, I've known she doesn't like Mason since forever ago, but everything else in her gaze is new to me. My eyes burn with the welling tears, one trickling down my cheek and turn to face the mirror while swiping it away.

"Why didn't you ever say anything?"

"Because you wouldn't have listened, Leighton. And when you first met him, his need to control you and your life was so subtle, even I missed it. Then, you were pregnant and getting married and thrilled with both." With a sigh, she places a hand on my shoulder and gives it a comforting squeeze. "By the time I realized how bad it truly was…"

As she trails off, I say, "I would've listened."

And the statement should've been said with confidence, but there's none to be found. We both know I wouldn't have listened to her because I remember that time in my life rather well. How I told myself I deserved the life I had because I chose it. I chose everything with Mason — to have children with him and tie myself to him forever.

But that's not the truth, now or then. He chose me, and I never saw the pain he would cause me coming until it was too late.

She doesn't say it; she doesn't have to. Instead, she slips her arm around the back of me and tugs me to her side as my tears start to flow. "You're my friend, Leighton, and damn, you're beautiful through and through. You always have been, and you don't see it, but that man out there? He does. He sees you as the woman you are, not the woman you've been pretending to be and fuck if I don't want to kiss him for it myself."

"So…" I shove the question through my sobs, hoping she gets what I mean. "You think he's worth the risk?"

"God, yes. But even if he weren't here, hon, if you were like this out of nowhere without his influence, I would tell you the same thing. Happiness — true and honest good with yourself and your life happiness — is always worth the risk. There's nobody in this world who's worth your health and sanity, and no man is worth your tears when he's the one making you cry."

"He's ten years younger than me." The words seem random as if I'm switching topics mindlessly, but in reality, I'm finally stating all the doubts I haven't acknowledged at all until now. "He's my daughter's teacher."

"He's hot."

"He is. He could also have anyone."

"He's with you. He wants you."

Even as I turn to glare at her, the final thought slips out in a soft, fearful expression of my uncertainties as they roll into one. "It could end badly."

Her gentle reply is at odds with the gleam in her eyes. "It could be everything a relationship should be and more."

I acknowledge her words with a nod, and after a few moments of staring at me as if she's trying to visualize what I'm not saying, she drags me back to the dining room. Back to Cole.

And all I can think the whole way is she probably wouldn't be happy to know what I wanted to reply to her last statement since it isn't a positive thing I know she desired to hear.

Since what I wanted to tell her is the relationship with Cole being everything and more is exactly what scares me most.

Because with it comes freedom which may cost me more than anything she or anyone else could imagine it might.

10

FOUR HOURS LATER, we've finished with dinner, and now we're sitting in a circle on the floor of April's room about to play poker.

Okay, strip poker specifically.

And by 'we' I mean me, Cole, April, and Jacob.

The card game was April's idea, and when she first suggested it thirty minutes ago, I came close to objecting, but all of them talked me into it.

April had glanced at Jacob with a naughty smirk and said with a laugh, "We're all adults here."

Cole caught my gaze and winked, leaning in from where he sat next to me to whisper, "I've already seen you naked plenty, babe. But I'll never turn down a harmless opportunity to do it more often."

I flushed, he pulled away after smacking his lips on mine in a smart-ass manner, and now, here we are about to start. Both April and I took off our shoes so everyone has the same clothing count, and April walks over to where we're sitting once she exits the bathroom.

Flouncing onto the floor, she produces the cards from her back pocket with a flourish, while Jacob makes us all our fourth drinks of the evening. Not used to drinking much, I'm already a bit tipsy, but at least it will make stripping down a bit easier.

She explains while dealing that it's not going to be a piece of clothing every hand. It's every time one of us folds or loses the hand. And before long, we're all drunk, laughing our asses off, and down to our underwear. I'm too drunk to be embarrassed, and not long after we started stripping Cole had moved closer until our knees were touching while making quite the show on keeping his cards hidden from me.

"Ooookay," April drawls as she throws her cards into the center and leans her head to rest on Jacob's shoulder while grinning. "I feel like now's a good…a good time to play truth or dare."

Cole tosses his cards in the center, putting his arm around me as I follow suit, and says, "Really? I haven't participated in that game since before high school."

Her smile is even brighter, turning naughty as she giggles and points a wobbly finger at me. "Yep. And she's first. Truth or dare, girl!"

My reply is a roll of my eyes along with a mumbled, "Truth."

"Of course. So, tell us, have you ever kissed a girl, and if so, who?"

Ah. I knew her game now. "You know damn well what the answer is."

"But Cole doesn't." Her laughter is pure amusement now as she gets on her hands and knees and crawls toward me until we're nose to nose. "So, tell us your answer."

"Nope."

She winks and both of us cast a glance at Cole, who watches us with open interest and a knowing smirk. "Why not?"

"Because you want to show him."

"I was the first girl she kissed." She informs Cole of something nobody else knows while staring at my mouth. "She came to college and was this sweet little innocent thing. We went to a party about a month in and drank, and this guy started hitting on her. She panicked, grabbed my arm to get my attention, and the moment I turned toward her, she leaned in and planted one right on my lips."

"Oh my god." My whole face flushes even as I grin at her. "I forgot about that! But he was such a creep!"

"Yep, he was, but you were even more shocked when I kissed you back. You pulled back and blushed just like you are now. It was so cute then and it still is now."

Knowing she's going to tell the whole story whether I want her to or not, I breathe out a small sigh and let her have her fun. "You tried to stick your tongue down my throat!"

The men start laughing, but it quickly ends when April leans in and presses her lips against mine, her tongue darting out to lick my mouth quick before she pulls away with a big smile. "I haven't seen you smile like this in so long. I'm truly happy for you, and well, it reminded me of that night."

"We had a good time."

"Yeah, we did." She sits back on her heels and lets out a loud yawn. "Well, I think it's time for bed. You two can sleep in the other room if you want. This suite is huge, and it's late, plus I think you're smashed."

"Right." Jacob joins in with a laugh, grabbing April's arm to help her as she stumbles to her feet. "You're not drunk at all, darling."

"Shhhhh."

They disappear into the other room and shut the door as Cole helps me stand up. The fact we both stumble while walking even a few steps means we're not going back to our room. Once we're in the spare April offered up, he shuts the door and it's not long before we're both passed out wrapped in each other's arms.

WAKING up next to Cole is different, and so good.

Cuddling with him after sex when we're together is nice, but it doesn't come close to comparing with him being the sight my eyes open up to after a night spent in the same bed.

Not a vision I get to appreciate for long because I need to pee, so I wiggle out from under his arm and am pleased to find a bathroom on the other side of the room, since it means I don't have to get dressed to go searching.

Surprisingly, I don't have a hangover, just feel a bit sluggish. Grimacing at my reflection while washing my hands, I pick up the tiny tube of toothpaste in the cup once my hands are clean, squirt some on my fingertip, and try to get rid of the bad aftertaste in my mouth. Doing it twice for good measure, I turn the water off, dry my hands, and then run them through my hair to make it a little more presentable.

Cole's sitting on the edge of the bed with his head in his hands as I walk out. Lifting to find me standing at the end, he smiles and runs his hand through his hair. "You don't look like your head hurts at all."

"It doesn't. Shocking since I'm sure I outdrank you all."

"Oh, I think April beat you there, but not by much." He pats the bed behind him. "Get back in and wait for me. I'll be back in a moment."

As he returns a few minutes later, he climbs in and under the blankets, snuggling up behind me.

"I feel like I've been waiting for this moment forever." He kisses the exposed nape of my neck, inhaling as if he can't get enough of me, and moves to nip at my earlobe with a soft chuckle as he admits, "That was also one of the best night's sleep I've ever gotten."

"Same here."

"Good. There's just one problem."

Turning in his arms, I wrap my arms around his

neck and smile up at him as he moves to cover his body with mine. "What's that?"

"We were too drunk last night to engage in the hours of sex I had planned."

"Well, we also didn't manage to make it back to our room."

"Time to see how quiet we can be." His suggestion is followed up with a kiss on the corner of my mouth. "Because I'm not waiting any longer to fuck you."

"Challenge accepted."

He moves enough to pinch my right nipple with his hand while his mouth sucks and nips at the other. At the same time, he glides his free hand down my body until he's cupping me between the legs. He groans while inserting two fingers inside me, he curls them to stroke my g-spot at the same time his naked form makes its descent down my body until both his hands are playing with my pussy as well as his mouth.

My back arches off the bed when he flicks his tongue over my clit, my hands flying from their grip on his hair to fist the sheets. Between the mix of his mouth and hands, the addition of his tongue plunging in and out in perfect rhythm has my whole body tightening as my orgasm crests, which seems stronger since I'm biting down on my lip to keep from crying out.

When he draws away, he gets up on his knees and gazes down at me, laughing at the face I make as he licks his lips in an exaggerated show of enjoyment. Then, in one smooth movement, he grasps my hips and yanks my body lower on the bed, skimming his hands toward my feet to straighten my legs until his face is between my feet. Sated, my hands keep their grip on the sheets as he grips my hips once more, lines up his cock to my pussy and then thrusts deep as he can go.

He starts off slow, but soon he's going fast and hard just like we both enjoy it, leaving me grateful the bed is so nice it doesn't make any noise to broadcast what we're doing. However, when Cole moves my legs to wrap around his waist and lowers his body while pressing his lips to mine, his moan is long, satisfied, and loud.

So powerful that as we're trying to catch our breaths, something hits the bedroom door a second before April's voice rings out. "God, quiet down in there, some of us have a hangover and can't have morning sex now!"

To say we laugh so hard we can't breathe isn't an overstatement at all.

11

WE'RE JUST ABOUT to order dinner when my phone dings.

Believing it's one of the kids simply checking in as I asked them to, I reach into my pocket and pull it out, only to see a message from Mason on my screen.

"Where the fuck are you?"

Grabbing Cole's arm in dismay, he turns his head with a confused look. "What's wrong?"

My phone dings again.

"This is what you do when I'm gone? Go somewhere without telling me first? Where the fuck are you and the kids Leigh?"

"Oh god." Tears pool in my eyes as Cole grabs the phone from me and reads the texts before cursing under his breath, making me feel the need to defend myself as April casts a concerned glance my way. "He's not supposed to be home. He said a week."

"Don't rush off," April says softly. "You're already here and having fun. Fuck him."

"I can't." I snatch my phone out of Cole's hand as another message arrives, standing up and pushing my chair in with an outward show of calm that belies my panic. "He'll find out where the kids are. They only have so many friends, and I can't...I gotta go."

April slams her hands on the table, making me flinch as she glares at me. "Listen to yourself. You can't what? Leave the kids alone with their father? Let me guess, they have no idea where you are either, so that makes you look guilty and will piss him off even more."

"April—" Cole starts to interrupt while rising, but stops when she holds up a hand while continuing to stare at me.

"You're my friend, and you're here with me at my request. My wedding is in two weeks. Text him and tell him that, along with how you'll be home tomorrow. You have the right to a life, Leighton."

"I know."

"Do you?" We stare at one another, her eyes flicking from my eyes to Cole and back to me, before dropping to my hands where I clutch my phone in my hand tightly. Lips twisting, she shakes her head and lifts her gaze to mine again, mouth flattening into a grim line. "Well, go on then. I can see there's no way you'll stay when he's still got his hooks in you."

With a brief look at Jacob, who is frowning up at an oblivious April, I whisper to her, "I'm sorry. I'll see you in two weeks."

She shrugs, hurting me more than even Mason could

at this moment, and drops her eyes as she sits back in her seat. "I'll believe that when I see it."

Whirling around on a hurt-filled gasp, tears blur my vision as I head toward the door at the same time Jacob snaps, "April!" I don't stay to hear what goes on after that though or wait for Cole to follow. I'm too focused on getting my stuff and checking out after texting him to say I'm on my way home that time passes in a blur, the fact Mason's now deprived me of my friend's respect driving my hatred even deeper.

But she doesn't understand. She just doesn't know everything and I don't have the heart to tell her.

I merely have to hope one day she'll forgive me for the choices I've made, and continue to make, to protect everything I hold dear.

THE DRIVE HOME with Cole is excruciating in its tenseness. I've never seen him act this way; his leg shakes, one hand clenched in a fist on his leg while the other rubs his forehead as he stares out the window.

Casting short glances his way every few seconds, I feel the need to say something, anything because he doesn't understand either. How could he? I haven't told him a thing.

"I know you don't understand—"

"Oh no." His words are flat and bitter as he doesn't even bother to look at me before responding. "I understand perfectly, Leighton, which makes me enraged more than you can possibly comprehend."

It's hard to focus on the road when he sounds so tortured, but the last thing I need is to get us into an accident I'd have to explain to Mason. "What do you mean?"

"Your expression when you read those texts. The fucking fear on your face, Leighton. We all saw it, and the way you jumped to do his bidding." He pauses to take a deep breath, his next question low and irate. " Goddammit, I need to know, is he hurting you?"

For a second, I wonder if he knows about my whole life with Mason but quickly toss it aside as impossible because he was a child himself when Mason and I got together.

Keeping my response light and airy, I laugh it off. "God no, Cole. He's neglectful, not abusive."

"I'm not Mason. Don't lie to me."

Jerking to look at him, I find him gazing at me with affection even though he's frowning. Making sure to take a quick glimpse back at the open highway in front of me, my eyes are on his as I state clearly and firmly, "I swear to you, he's not physically abusive. He's… he's just a fucking asshole sometimes, all right?"

He waits until I look at the road and back at him again before he nods, then states, "All the time."

"Yes, dammit. All the time." Tearing my eyes from him, I lock my eyes on the road. "If he weren't, we wouldn't even be together right now to have this conversation, and you know it."

One rough exhalation later, the gentle touch of his left hand on my thigh as he rests it there, the one question I never expected from him falling from his lips. "Why do you stay?"

My mouth opens to answer, yet nothing comes out, and I snap it shut again.

There're so many ways to answer his question, yet only one of them would be the truth. Everything else is pure deception; the mask I put on a long time ago and rarely take off even when around Cole. It's the same one April broke through for an instant with her perceptions, weakening a small part of me which aches for the freedom it will never be granted.

So to avoid baring the soul of me, the part I've been hiding for so long I'm not even sure it exists anymore, I give him an answer in a roundabout way.

"When we first met, he charmed me. He was funny, smart, and gentle. We didn't get married because I was pregnant; he asked me before then, bringing up having children sooner rather than later even. 'I want to enjoy my children and have enough energy to enjoy my old age,' he'd said to me, and I agreed with him. No point in waiting, right, since he had a job waiting.

"We got married and it was fantastic. 'Til death do us part and happily ever after, that's what I promised him. On our wedding day, he held my hand tight as he put that ring on, and for the rest of the ceremony. It's like once I wore it, I was his, and I wasn't even to leave his side.

For the first two years of our marriage, I couldn't

even go out shopping without him. He would insist I wait until he was off work to even get groceries, so everything had to be planned perfectly. I couldn't forget anything or a meal would be messed up."

My fingers tighten on the steering wheel. "The first time I did, I just panicked. I knew if I told him what was for dinner, and he came home to something different, he'd be so angry. I went to the store and back as fast as I could, wasn't even an hour, but when he got home, somehow he knew."

"Leighton—"

I cut in, not wanting to hear what he has to say to that as I rush ahead. "He hinted at it until I broke down and confessed to what I had done, and that's when he smiled. He walked to where I stood, took me in his arms, and stroked his hand down my hair whispering, 'It's okay, Leigh. You did such a good job today, you can go out when I'm not around since I know it's inconvenient. Just know you're mine. Nobody is allowed to touch you. Forsaking all others, remember? I love you and you're mine forever. Don't forget it.' His words were soft, but he held me so tight I knew he could just as easily steal my breath. I've never forgotten it, word for word."

"Jesus." He falls silent, then says after a few moments, "There is no such thing as happy ever after, Leighton, you know that right? Because in the end, we're all gonna die."

"That's morbid."

"It's only morbid because it's a fact nobody can deny."

"So, what?"

"What are you waiting for? One day, you're going to die. It can either be while living the rest of your life in your marriage with a man who has zero respect for you, or you can leave and find what happiness you can elsewhere."

"And what is happiness exactly? Starting a new life filled with uncertainty after I've spent more than a decade being nothing more than a housewife and mother?"

"I can't tell you what to do, babe—"

I direct a glare his way while raising my voice to convey my mounting frustration. "Why not? If you and April have all the answers, why not give them to me, instead of telling me to make a choice I obviously have chosen not to make in the last fifteen years?"

He slaps his hand on the dashboard, causing me to flinch as he admits to his real thoughts. "Fine. I believe you should leave him. If you were happy, if he fulfilled your needs, you wouldn't be so fucking unhappy. You wouldn't be with me at all."

My laugh is pure disbelief as I focus on the road, my chest tightening with the truth of his words, fighting for recognition at the same time I tamp them down. "Two weeks since that first night, and that's it? I should end my stable marriage for you?"

"Goddammit, that's not what I said—"

"So you don't want that?" I'm aware of the fact I'm acting childish. However, it's all I can do to contain my anxiety right now and pay attention to the road while my denial of how my life actually is takes over.

"Fuck, babe, I will take you any way I can get you. Whatever makes you happy. Do you want more?" Heart skipping at his question, all the things I want collide with all the things I've had to do for all these years just to survive. Because of it all, the only answer I'm able to give him is a sad shrug. "Maybe it's too soon for you to answer that. So, tell me this. Is this—what we have right now—is it good enough for you?"

My response is the first time I'll ever straight out tell a lie to Cole. Taking the exit ramp leading into the downtown area and stopping at the red light, my lie's made worse by the fact he looks me straight in the eyes as I jerk my gaze to his. I hate myself as I force the distasteful words past my lips. "Yes, it is."

What I don't say is, "Because it has to be."

After a few scrutinizing seconds, he nods as if accepting my lie even though I know he sees right through it. Snatching my hand up with his, he draws it toward his mouth and places a gentle kiss on my knuckles.

Just as quick, he lets go without another word and proceeds to turn away to stare out the window once more.

Pressing the gas as the light turns green, I clench my right hand as if doing so will hold onto the sensation of his lips against my skin while the strange feeling of his motion meaning something enters my mind. As if he were trying to tell me something important.

But the relief of not fighting with him, of knowing he has no intentions of giving our relationship up, has the thought flitting away as fast as it arrived.

AFTER DROPPING Cole off at his place, which involved him giving me a slow and sweet kiss goodbye, I take my time getting home. Not in a rush to hear Mason's mouth, I stop at the grocery store and pick up some things for dinner I had planned on getting tomorrow, and let out a sigh of relief when I arrive home to find Mason not there. Not that it eases my anxiety because I know he'll be back with the kids if he went to go get them as he said he was after my final text to him earlier.

Carrying in the groceries, I start a pot of water for the spaghetti, put the meat into the frying pan to brown, and put some sauce in a saucepan to heat up once the water is boiling for the noodles. Having set the table, I walk back into the kitchen as the water boils rapidly, and at the same moment the back door opens.

Dean and Jenna walk past first, both mumbling 'hi' with their heads down as they head to their rooms, and the fact their dejection is obvious pisses me off. Having him ruin our whole weekend by not being on his trip like he said he would be, made worse by him picking them up from their friends' house as if they've done something wrong, is enough for my caution to get thrown to the wind before I've even thought about the consequences of speaking up.

"What the hell is your problem?"

Mason pauses in the doorway, head jerking up to pin me with an incredulous countenance. "I don't have a problem, Leigh, and I'd advise you watch what you say to me right now."

Feeling brave in a way I haven't in a while, my response is snide. "Or what? You'll pick me up from my friend's house when I've done nothing wrong just to demonstrate how big and bad you are?"

His expression turns thunderous as he steps inside, slams the door with a pronounced bang, and walks toward me in what I can only describe as a lethal manner. The counter slams into my lower back as he corners me against it, one arm on each side of my body as he says in a tight voice, "I'm sorry, I must've misheard you just now. Care to repeat what you said?"

Taking a deep breath, my reply is soft and steady although my heart beats faster than ever before. "There was no reason for you to go get them tonight. They were only staying until tomorrow."

I hate the way his voice lowers as he leans in, breathing on my ear while keeping me captive with his body. "And where were you that you weren't supposed to be, Leigh?"

"At April's pre-wedding get together, which was at the hotel close to where she's getting married." He relaxes a little until I continue with, "Which you would've known had you bothered to ask instead of rushing out of town with that girl you're fucking."

Leaning in toward me, his eyes narrow while his hand comes up to rest just below my neck, the pad of his thumb stroking in a way meant to intimidate me. "Yes, that reminds me, what the fuck did you say to Wendy when I left the room?"

"You should just tell me what she said since you're going to believe her over me anyway."

"I'm not in the mood for your fucking games, Leigh."

"My games?" With a laugh, I lift my arms and do something I've never dared to do before, shoving my hands against his shoulders hard until he stumbles back. "You're the one bringing your fuck buddy to dinner with your family!"

If I weren't so furious, his murderous glare might scare me, but I stand here waiting in cold anticipation for him to react. I learned a long time ago that if Mason is upset, it doesn't matter what I do or say, he'll react anyway. I'm not sure what to expect though because it's been years since I talked to him like this, yet it still shocks me when he grabs the hot saucepan from the stove and throws it across the room.

Then as the sauce splashes all over the wall and drips down to the floor, he pivots on his heel, snatches his keys off the hook, and exits the house without another word.

Leaving me to look at the mess all over the other side of the kitchen that I now have to clean up before it stains, and the faces of Dean and Jenna, eyes wide and filled with fear as they arrive to see what happened.

Although I feel like crying, another part of me can't help feeling a bit of pride in myself for standing up to him, and relief that his only retaliation was to throw a pan before walking out.

Tears do spring to my eyes when Jenna heads over to the closet, grabs the mop bucket, and begins to fill it with water while Dean walks to where I'm standing, wraps his arms around my waist, and says, "It's okay, Mom. Now we can order pizza instead."

It's enough to break the anxiety we're all experiencing, both Jenna and me laughing with Dean joining in after a moment. And once I've shut off the rest of the food and cleaned up the sauce, order pizza for the three of us is exactly what I do.

By the time I head to bed, Mason once again hasn't returned home, and my only thought on that is how that's just fine with me.

12

WHEN JENNA'S not waiting out in front of the school after tutoring, I park the car in the closest spot and head inside, wondering if her session ran late.

It's been four days since my argument with Mason in the kitchen, and beyond him having more of an attitude when talking to me, there's been no mention of it. He leaves for working early in the morning, and if it weren't for the fact his head leaves an imprint in the pillow next to me, I wouldn't know he even came home since he's gone before I wake up.

Turning down the hall toward Mister Graham's room, the sound of a whistle and feet running across the gym makes me pause when I reach the doorway and look inside in hopes of catching a glimpse of Cole.

Almost as if he knows I'm standing here, he looks up at the same time my eyes land on him, and after telling the kids something I can't make out, he jogs over to me. Stopping in front of me, he makes sure to keep a good distance even as his gaze checks me out from head to toe, the resulting grin matching the hunger in his eyes.

"Looking good as always babe." His comment is hushed as he tosses a look over his shoulder to make sure the kids are doing what they were told before facing me again. "Here to pick up Jenna?"

"Yeah. She wasn't outside, though. Came in to see if her tutoring session is running late or what."

He frowns, running a hand through his hair before shaking his head, and crosses his arms over his chest. "I saw him walk past my door about five minutes ago with his briefcase, so it's likely he's gone already."

"Oh."

"She's probably in the restroom and got caught up in talking with one of her friends or something." He lifts his left hand a little and points to the left with his thumb. "It's just down the hall."

"Okay, I will check there. Thanks." Taking a step back, I nod at the kids behind him. "What's this? Are you in charge of another sport I don't know of?"

"No. Detention." He laughs, dropping his arms to his sides and curling his hands into fists. "Administration decided it's more of a punishment than making them sit in a classroom. Recent decision."

"Is it working?"

"Yep. Well, there's a few stubborn kids who don't seem to care, but otherwise, nobody's been here twice."

"Good." With a pointed look at his hands, I lift a brow and grin. "Having a problem?"

He winks and smiles back at me. "It's hard as hell to

avoid touching you or pulling you into my arms for a hug."

I know exactly how he feels, pursing my lips to mimic a kiss, and then flash him a smile brimming with promise. "Later."

"Looking forward to it."

"Me too." I take another step back and turn toward the left. "See you then."

He waves me off and goes back to the kids with a blow of his whistle, while I head down the hall, keeping an eye out for the bathroom as my thoughts roam to how nice it'll be to see Cole this evening. He always seems to make everything better, and I wonder how long it'll last because Mason used to make me feel the same way.

Sighing with relief as the sign comes into view, I walk right in once I reach it since it's one of those without an exterior door, and stop at the wall that separates the entrance way from the row of stalls while calling out for her.

"Are you in here, Jenna?" At the silence, I'm sure there's no one in here until I hear a muffled sniffle that makes me step inside to see who's crying. "Hello? Are you okay?"

After a second, the stall furthest from the door opens, and Jenna steps out with red eyes and a tissue held to her nose. My immediate instinct is to examine her from head to toe, but the only problem with her that I can see is her crying.

"Honey, what's wrong?"

"Nothing." She blows her nose, tosses the tissue in the trash and walks toward me. "I just had a bad day."

Remembering how someone grabbed her all those weeks ago makes it necessary I try to get to the bottom of what her bad day consisted of. "Bad day how? Did that boy grab you again?"

She laughs, shrugging out of reach of my hand as she walks past me to the sink and washes her hands. "Can we just go home, please?"

"Jenna—"

Looking me straight in the eye for the first time, her lips wobble as her whole face starts to crumple and she begs, "Please, Mom. Just don't say anything else, and take me home okay? I don't feel good."

It's hard for me not to continue to try to get her to talk to me, but I do as she asks, especially since this is the first time in a while I've seen any emotion other than anger from her.

The whole car ride to pick up Dean, and then home, is completely quiet between all of us. Once we arrive, Jenna jets out of the car as if she can't get away from me fast enough, making it clear I won't be going out for a ride this evening because there's no way I can leave her brother here with her like this.

Sending Cole a text message telling him Jenna's not doing well so I have to cancel, it's nice to receive a perfectly understanding message in return from him, telling me maybe tomorrow with a smile and he hopes she's better by tomorrow.

It's a far cry from the way Mason reacts to me telling

him about it as he climbs into bed later that evening, blowing it off as 'teenage girl hormones' before rolling over and falling asleep in minutes.

For the second night this week, he leaves me wishing I had the guts to smother him with a damn pillow. Instead, I get out of bed and check on Dean first, then Jenna. And once I see her sound asleep in her bed, it makes it easier to go back to my own and get some rest as well while hoping tomorrow is a better day.

THE FOLLOWING WEEK, Mason decides at the last minute that he will be attending April's wedding with me. So he doesn't dress until I'm nearly ready to go, which means we're nearly thirty minutes late upon arrival.

Good thing she wanted me there an hour before the ceremony.

As we walk in, I can tell the fact Mason is there isn't something she expects, but he doesn't know her like I do. A good thing since that means he misses the disgusted grimace she makes before pasting a smile on her face as we approach.

"Leighton, you're late, but that's okay." She takes hold of my hand as she greets him. "Mason, nice to see you. You can go ahead inside and take a seat. I need Leighton to help me change for the ceremony. We're a little behind."

With a nod to her and a look of warning for me, he walks toward the banquet room and leaves us alone.

April doesn't speak, dragging me down the hallway, and shutting the door behind us once we're in the room with her dress. Dropping my hand, she walks over to the mirror and starts stripping, grabbing her dress and stepping into it before addressing me.

"I'm sorry about the last time, Leighton. I had no right to tell you what to do with your marriage."

"It's okay. You're not entirely wrong. It's just complicated."

"I know." She pulls the straps over her shoulders, indicating with a swipe of her hand up and down her back that I need to come over and zip it. "But even if I think that way, I shouldn't make you feel bad for what you do. The fact you're seeing another man is a step in the right direction."

For some reason, her statement amuses me, and I laugh while stepping up behind her to finish helping her into the dress. "Like I said, it's okay. You wanted me to stay, rightfully, and I know you don't understand, but I made the right choice that day. He went and picked up the kids from their friends even though there was no good reason for him to do it."

"What?" She scowls and turns around once I step back, shaking her head before walking over to the vanity and picking up her lipstick. "He's such a cocksucker. I'm only nice to him because of you."

If she only knew the whole of it. "I'm aware and I appreciate it."

"How are the kids anyway? Doing well in school?"

"Dean is, but not Jenna. She's struggling, and I can't figure out why. She's not exactly forthcoming." I fill her in on that day at the school, and how Jenna returned to being her grumpy, unapproachable self since then and give her a sad smile when she frowns. "I'm sure it's just her age, but I don't remember being that moody at thirteen."

"Who does?" Laughing, she turns away once her lipstick is on and slips on her bracelets. "Is it possible she's being bullied by other girls or even boys? High school is ripe for that sort of stuff."

"Maybe. All I know is, whatever it is, she's channeling it at school in general. She doesn't want to go in the morning, she hates her tutoring session with the math teacher who she refers to as an asshole, and all her grades are slowly slipping. I'm at a complete loss as to what to do."

"Damn. Maybe it's time to get her to a psychiatrist. She might be depressed."

"That's the thing, we've done that too. They have her on anti-depressants, and a sleeping pill cause she says otherwise she can't sleep at night. But I don't think either is helping her."

"I'm sorry" She embraces me in her arms to hug me close, tightly, before drawing away and smiling. "I'm sure it doesn't help that her father's a dick, but there ya have it."

"Ha."

"There's a smile. Good." Turning away, she stalks

toward the door and opens it while grabbing her veil. "Now keep it on your face, help me put this on, and let's go so I can finally fucking get married!"

Even as I do as she bids, the small part of me that has experienced getting married and everything that comes with it has to hold back, hoping this isn't the happiest moment of her marriage with Jacob, like it is in regard to my marriage.

Hard as it is, I shove the thought away and once her veil is on, fluff her skirts before saying, "Okay, all done."

Her laughter as we enter the hallway might be from the unexpected smack on her ass delivered by me as I shut the door, joining in with her as she loops her arm through mine.

The minutes alone with her end up setting the mood for the rest of the evening, one, not even Mason's icy attitude can ruin. And when the preacher announces Jacob and April as man and wife, I try not to compare the happiness on their faces to the lack of my own, telling myself there's nothing to compare to.

Lying to myself is what I do to get through my life, after all.

13

"I HATE SEEING YOU GO." Cole lies on the bed behind me, naked and wet as he watches me getting dressed in the mirror after our quick after sex shower. "Every time you do, I fear it will be the last evening you're in my arms."

Laughing, I catch his gaze through the mirror while reaching back to clasp my bra. "And miss out on the amazing sex with you? Not a chance."

He moves fast, standing behind me in a blink, one hand on each of my upper arms as mine fall to my sides, and he stares at me with an intense expression. "We're more than sensational sex."

Lifting his left hand, he moves my hair away from my neck and presses his lips to the crook of my shoulder, then lifts his eyes as he grins against my skin. "It's too bad I can't mark your skin the same way you mark mine."

My smile matches his. "I do enjoy it."

"I know." Skimming his mouth along my neck, the feel of his teeth gliding along the sensitive area leaves tingles in their wake, and he wraps his arms around me after witnessing my shivering response. "I'll miss you."

It's the same ending to our time together as always when I remind him, "I will too, but you'll see me in a few days."

"Monday night. Three days too long."

"But better than never again." I remind him while turning in his hold and wrapping my arms around his neck. "I have to get going. I'm going to be late at this rate."

As one of his hands slips to cup my ass, the other slides up to my neck and around back, both bringing me forward with a little force from his hold until his mouth covers mine in a kiss which comforts me and turns me on simultaneously. I let his tongue in when he seeks entrance, moaning when he grinds our lower bodies together, and wish I didn't have to go anywhere.

Even though he hasn't mentioned our relationship becoming anything more than this since our time at the hotel, it's something I do think about every time we're together, and every time I'm on my way home from being with him. I wonder what it would be like for us to date openly, to get to know one another outside of our secret evenings, and whether we would survive as a couple.

But then Mason sneaks into my thoughts. How he is, how he would react, if he would retaliate against me asking for a divorce; it all factors in to why I remain silent. And yes, I'm a little sad, but I'm protecting myself as much as shielding Cole because he doesn't know Mason like I do, nor what he's capable of.

And that's what I think of to make myself drag my lips away, take a step back, and clear my throat while glancing around for my jeans. "Really have to get going."

"YOU'RE LATE."

Mason's voice rises from the darkness as I walk past the living room, causing me to freeze in place almost immediately because he's home earlier than expected. Turning to face his direction even though I can't quite see him, I stumble over my words and give away a little of my fear. "I'm... I'm sorry. I—"

"Stop." The angrily spoken word is like a vicious lash of a whip in the air, cutting me off as he suddenly appears right in front of me. His breathing is harsh as he questions me like I've dreaded for weeks now. "Where have you been, Leigh?"

I force myself to stay calm, to keep my voice a reasonable tone as I answer him. "Riding my bike, just like I told you when I texted you earlier."

"And what? You lost track of time?"

Obviously I hadn't, but he also hasn't been home, so I hadn't expected him to be waiting for me upon arriving home. I won't say that, though, answering instead with a simple, "Yes."

The soft glow of the hallway light shines down on both of us as we stand there. Mason lifts his hand, his face softening as he places one hand under my chin and tilts it up, holding it there as his equally bright gaze stares into mine.

"Don't lie to me." His grip on my chin tightens, only to loosen it when I whimper, and he drops his hand. "Tell me why you're late."

I keep my face neutral, blinking normally, as I have for years now to hide any personality traits he doesn't like. I know I'm good at lying; I've been doing it for so long now it is second nature when I'm around him. "I've told you, Mason. It was so nice out, it was late before I knew it. I came back as soon as I realized—"

"Where are the children, Leigh?"

The sudden question and change of topic catches me off guard, and I blink rapidly, recovering just as quickly to smile softly at him. "They are both spending the weekends with their friends. I sent you a message, remember? I—"

"Go upstairs."

I hate that he cuts me off, but even more so, I hate his ordering me around like this. I know he'll listen if I just stay calm and rational, showing no emotion because that pisses him off the most.

"All right," I say with a nod, because this isn't worth the fight anyway, and turn toward the steps.

"Leigh?"

Taking as deep a breath as I can without him seeing

or hearing it, I turn back to him with a smile meant to appease him. "Yes?"

"I hate when you lie to me." His voice is deceptively soft as he speaks, eyes filled with disappointment, and for a moment, I wonder if I should be ashamed of what I've done. "You should know better than to think I'd believe you for one fucking second."

His face contorts with rage, going from the man with the natural smile to the tormentor I haven't seen in a long time in an instant.

It's been so long, I've forgotten the signs, or even the need to watch out for them. I don't even see the first slap coming until it's too late, my ears ringing as my head snaps to the side with the force of the blow.

And then, ah…I remember what comes next as terror fills my heart.

"Please, Mason." The words are pleading, begging, and even though I know it will only make things worse, the words pour from my mouth unbidden. "Please, don't. I'm sorry."

Worthless words as he hits me again, causing me to stumble to the side yet not hard enough to make me fall.

Nine years it's been since he's laid a hand on me.

Nine years since I got on my knees before him and swore I'd never do anything to upset him again if he would not hit me, for the sake of raising our children together.

Nine years of me being the perfect wife and the perfect mother down the drain due to my forgetfulness.

How could I fuck up like this? How could I be so

careless? I knew the consequences of any deception and now he'll make me pay the price.

I fall to my knees, the words pleading for his forgiveness and mercy bursting forth, but it's too late.

Tonight, there will be none given by him, because his rage is too far gone.

When he grabs my hair, yanking it as hard as he can, I force myself to give in and take what's coming to me without making a sound because fighting only makes him angrier.

Only this time while he assaults me with his hands and belt, I'm far away emotionally, safe and sound in the loving arms of Cole.

Thinking it's time to find a way out for me and my children as I should've done years ago, as fast as I can manage before the ticking time box that is Mason blows up in my face.

"MOM?" Jenna's voice is hushed as she enters the relatively dark bedroom, approaching the bed as quietly as she can, and I feel her touch my side through the blankets. I control the urge to wince, but just barely as she asks, "Do you need anything? Some soup or something?"

"No, but thank you, honey." I can't manage anything more than a whisper, staying still as possible, and force myself to yawn loudly. "I'm about to go back to sleep. I'm tired."

"Dad says you've been sick since Friday night and wouldn't let us come in here all weekend. Are you still sick?"

If I had any tears left in me, I would cry. "Yes, honey, but I'm getting better. You should go before you catch it too. Have a good day at school, okay? And tell Dean I'm all right too so he doesn't worry, please."

"Okay." When I feel her lean toward my face, I close my eyes, and she presses a sweet kiss to my cheek. "Love you, Mom."

"Love you too."

She leaves the room as quietly as she entered.

Lying there listening, I wait for the sound of the door below to shut. When the garage door opens and closes — indicating Mason's left with the kids to take them to school and head to work — I toss aside the blankets.

Because I hurt all over, it takes a moment for me to sit up, and then actually stand up, but I manage it. Walking slowly, I eventually make it to the bathroom, shutting the door behind me before turning to look at myself in the mirror.

There's only a small bruise by the corner of my left eye from where he slapped me across the face, but it's barely noticeable. Except for just the one time years ago, he's always been too smart to leave marks where anybody could see them, and this time is no exception.

Even as I take off my robe and lower my nightgown, the mirror only confirms what I already know as I turn around. Looking over my shoulder, the crisscross of welts from Mason's belt have my eyes tearing up as they haven't in days. Some of them curl around the edges, especially around my waist, and they go all the way down to my ass. The good thing is it doesn't look bad and no broken skin; the bad thing is they are quite painful, yet I know I have to move around to keep my back from stiffening up.

It's going to be a rough day for me.

Stripping completely, I walk over to the shower and turn it on, making sure the water is as hot as I can handle before stepping inside. The water pelts down on me, making me cry out in pain at first. Although I manage to keep from screaming like I want to, I eventually manage to work past the discomfort of lifting my arms so I can wash my hair.

It seems as if the whole process is exceedingly slow, but after a bit, I finish my hair and wash my body. Getting out as the water starts to cool, even with the hot turned all the way up, I dry off as gently as I can and put on the softest shirt and pajama pants I can find.

Twenty-odd minutes later, my mind wanders as I head into the kitchen and put a bagel in the toaster. Other than my kids, Cole's all I've thought about all weekend. I know he's probably worried since he hasn't heard from me in two days, which is a departure from when I texted him every chance I got since he gave it to me. Even if I could force myself to go back up the steps right now — which I really don't want to, honestly — it wouldn't matter because I know he's at work anyway.

I have to make sure to text him before Mason gets home, at least, and make up some reason why we can't see each other for a bit. I absolutely don't want or need Cole to see me like this; it's hard knowing how he would react, but if he goes after Mason, that's not what I want at all. This whole thing needs to be handled carefully, not with violence, which is the very thing I wish to escape.

My bagel pops up in the toaster at the same time the doorbell rings. I consider ignoring it, but once it rings again almost as if the person is pushing the button violently, I sigh and shuffle as fast as I can to see who it is.

Shocked doesn't even begin to describe how I feel when I see Cole's face staring back at me through the peephole. I consider pretending as if I'm not awake or something, but he puts a stop to that immediately.

"Leighton, open up. I know you're in there. Let me in before I let myself in, and you don't wanna know how I'll manage that."

Oh, I've no doubt he'll break down my door to get to me now.

Tears spring to my eyes as I realize he's going to discover what I've been hiding for way too long now, but I know I can't deny him when he's on my doorstep.

And the truth is, as I now admit to myself, I don't want to. I want him to know; he needs to see what I'm dealing with because, at this point, I'm not sure I'll be able to get away without help. He just has to know he can't go after Mason, not unless he wants to make things worse.

So with that in mind, I take a deep breath, unlock

the deadbolt and twist the knob before stepping back as I open the door.

Cole smiles at the sight of me, quickly dissipating as his eyes widen in horror at the small bruise on my face, and anger swiftly takes over his features.

He steps inside, slams the door behind him, and shakes his head as his hands curl into fists at his sides. "That fucking son of a bitch is about to take his last breath."

14

COLE PACES BACK and forth in front of the sink as I sit at the table eating breakfast, which he'd insisted on completing the preparation of. He shoves a hand through his hair in an aggravated fashion, since I've told him he can't go after Mason, and I know this is just the beginning.

As I finish my food, he leans back against the counter with his arms crossed over his chest and focuses all his attention on me. "Show me what else he did, sweetheart."

"Cole—"

He walks over to me, placing a hand on my shoulder as gentle as possible, instantly removing his hand when I wince and gritting his teeth. "Fuck! Take off your shirt, Leighton. Please."

"No." When I stand up he backs off a little, but I simply stand there with my back facing him, and whisper, "Just lift very gently and look. I had enough trouble getting it on."

It doesn't take long for his hands to start trembling as he lifts my shirt and uncovers my back, his sharp breath punctuated by a quiet, tortured sounding moan. "Oh god, babe..." He drops my shirt, commanding in a soft tone, "Turn around."

He opens his arms when I do as he bids, and I wrap mine around his waist, unexpected sobs bursting forth as his come up to my neck. Cradling my head with one, he caresses the nape of my neck with the fingertips of his other hand. He lowers his head until it rests lightly on top of mine, which is weird for me yet comforting at the same time.

"We've got to get you out of here," he declares after a few moments of us standing there hugging like that. "You, Jenna, and Dean can't stay here any longer."

"No." I shake my head, well as much as I can with him holding me like he is and say the rest through my sniffles. "It's not that easy. He controls everything — the money, the house, the car; everything is in his name. I have nowhere safe to take me or the kids—"

"You have me," he cuts in almost desperately. "Come stay with me."

I go to pull away, and he lets me go smoothly, sliding his hands into his pockets as I tell him, "You? It's hardly appropriate to go stay with another man when I'm leaving their father and we barely know each other Cole—"

He holds up a hand, staring at me with distress clear

on his face. Then, his voice drops low, his confused expression matching his tone as he asks, "You don't know who I am, do you?"

Now I'm the one at a loss as his question baffles me. "Of course I know who you are. You're Cole Vaughn, my daughter's gym teacher, and more recently, my lover."

His mouth drops open for a few seconds before snapping shut as he shoves his hand through his hair again, starting to pace back and forth once more. "Fuck. You don't fucking know! Shit, shit!" He slaps his hand down on the counter when he stops walking, which causes me to jump a little, and stares right at me with amazement. "How do you not know who I am?"

"You're not making any sense, and you're scaring me."

"Sorry." He walks over to the table and pulls out a chair. "I think you should sit down for this."

Even though I'm still really dumbfounded and not understanding what he's going on about, I do as he says, and he takes a seat across from me. Clasping his hands together with his elbows on the table, he closes his eyes as he begins speaking.

"Nine years ago, I was sixteen. Me, my stepfather, my mother, and my three siblings were all at the grocery store. As we finished shopping, we headed toward our car, and it was pouring down rain. My siblings ran ahead to the car, laughing and dancing in the rain while the three of us just walked as we normally do, getting soaked but we didn't care. It was the middle of the day, and suddenly, I looked over to the right because I heard crying. At first, I thought it was just a kid."

If he hears my breath hitch, he ignores it and keeps on talking.

"Then I realized it wasn't just a kid. This woman stood with the back of her car open, sobbing while two children in the car wailed for her, and just as we passed by, she dropped a bag on the ground. And all I could hear then was the sound of her crying harder and swearing like a sailor. I ran over to help, but she'd bent down to do something and the glasses on her face fell off.

She didn't realize I was there, though, because she swept the glasses up off the ground, and stood up without putting them back on. When she finally saw me standing a few feet away, she shoved the glasses back on, but by then it was too late. I saw the black eye she was sporting and called out to my stepdad."

I don't need or want to hear anymore as my stomach heaves almost painfully. "Cole—"

"No." He opens his eyes up and leans forward, eyes glinting with anger as he stares at me. "I knew who she was, and so did my stepdad. I helped her get the rest of the things in the car. Meanwhile, my mother ran back in and got the woman some more eggs after she cried she was only allowed to spend so much and couldn't afford to replace them." He reaches across the table and snatches my hand in his, holding it tight. "My father asked her how she got the black eye, and she spouted off some bullshit about walking into a wall because she wasn't watching where she was going."

I lower my head, my gaze falling to my lap as tears fill my eyes. He keeps talking though because he knows I remember. It's a day I'll never forget.

"My mother came back out, gave you the eggs, along with a card with our number on it so you could call us if you needed to. If you needed help. You never called." He pauses and says, "Look at me." When I lift my teary gaze, he gives me a tender smile. "He didn't come home that night, did he?"

I think back for a second before shaking my head in response. "No. He... he called me and said he had a sudden business trip. Didn't return until two weeks later."

Cole releases a sharp bark of laughter. "Oh yeah, a sudden business trip. That's because that fucker got the shit beat out of him for touching you and told if he ever did it again, he'd be in deep shit." When I gasp and stare at him wide eyed, his mouth thins into a straight line. "You never knew this? He never told you what happened? Why am I not surprised."

"I don't know. Maybe he planned to, but he came home from the trip and I was so desperate to have him never do that again, I promised him I'd do whatever it took. But... why would you care? I—"

"Leighton. You know who my stepdad is right?" He laughs as if it's the funniest thing ever when I stare at him blankly. "My god. My stepfather is David Whitfield. He's—"

Now it's my turn to cut in, my words coming out in a horrified whisper as I yank my hand from his. "Oh... oh, my god! He's Mason's boss. You're David Whitfield's son?"

"Babe." His whole expression fills with hurt at my pulling away, but he doesn't try to grab my hand again. "How could you not know who I was when you ran into me? I thought you knew this whole time."

I can't even focus on him. All I keep thinking is how I'm having an affair with my husband's boss' son, and suddenly I feel sick. So sick, and in so much pain I can't move fast enough to hide in the bathroom.

"Oh god. I'm... I'm gonna be sick."

He leaps up, and seeing an empty mixing bowl on the counter, grabs it. He shoves it in my hands just in time as I throw up my breakfast. I'm horrified he's there while this is happening, but this is all his fault, and I can't fucking move.

He puts the bowl in the sink for me when it's over as I ask him, "If you thought I knew who you were, why did you pretend not to know me in the school?"

"I thought you were the one pretending," he says with a snort of disbelief. "Figured you were playing it safe by acting like you didn't recognize me or my name."

I'm even more confused now as I recall the day at the school. "You asked me if we had met before."

"To see if you would say you knew me or keep acting like you didn't. When you didn't tell me you were joking, I played along."

"I'm sorry," I tell him with a frown. "I'm thinking back to the day in the rain when I really wasn't focused on anything but how panicked I was. And the times we had the get-together every summer for all the employees and their families? I don't... I don't remember seeing you." My nose tingles with the urge to cry. I've spent the last nine years of my life 'out of it,' so much I missed important details I didn't even know I needed. "Maybe it was your last name. It must've thrown me off because I knew you all as the Whitfield's. I even remember Mason referring to a Cole, but maybe I missed the fact you were his stepson? We didn't talk, did we?"

"No, I didn't attend the get-togethers, but I thought you knew I was his son. I'm the one who's sorry. I should've made sure you knew instead of assuming." He stops talking and stands up with a determined look on his face. "Know what? It doesn't matter now. You know who I am now, and you need to let me help you. Let me and my family get you away from him."

"I can't." I hold up a hand as he steps forward and his frown deepens as I point toward the door. "I... you should go. I have to think."

"Leighton—"

"Please," I plead with him, taking his hands in mine and giving them a squeeze as I stare at him, frowning. "Please go. And leave Mason alone. I promise I'm gonna leave him, but I need... I need to work out some things myself first. Okay?"

He doesn't look too happy with anything I've just said, but after staring at me long and hard he sighs, relenting. "Okay, fine. Just promise me if you need me, you'll text me and you'll be careful. Also, know if you don't contact me at least once a day, there will be cops knocking down your fucking door in an instant."

Sniffling, I nod in agreement as he leans in, pressing a kiss to my forehead before walking over to the door. He cast me one more look over his shoulder before turning the knob and leaving me alone once more, wondering what the hell kind of mess I've gotten myself into.

And how I'm going to get myself out of it while hoping Mason doesn't find out exactly what's been going on between me and Cole.

15

MASON ARRIVES home at six again this evening as he has this whole week, and just as he walks in, I place the last item for dinner on the table.

It's been two weeks since he assaulted me and the marks on my back have completely vanished.

He acts as if it never happened, and his pattern now follows the one from all those years ago. He's being super nice and doing things to help around the house as if that makes up for what he's done. He hasn't said sorry, and I haven't forgiven him, but that doesn't matter.

I've tried to act as if everything's okay, but I know I'm failing.

It's not okay, I want out, and the way he's starting to suffocate me indicates he can feel it.

After all, we've been together for sixteen years, and nine of those I've spent hiding behind a wall of perfection to avoid upsetting him. Only now I know it's all been nothing but a big, fat lie.

Mason is a coward, and he only stopped touching me to save his own ass. He knew they had their eyes on him, and on me, which is the only reason he quit hitting me, except he let me believe it was all due to the fact I had begged him so sweetly.

I should've known better than to think it had anything to do with loving me and wanting to make things right between us. And if I'm truly honest with myself, the fact I've been the Leighton he wants instead of the authentic version of myself all these years says it all. Not that me promising him to be perfect kept him from abusing me in different ways, like isolating me from my family and controlling my every move.

God, I've been so blind for quite a long time to everything, but I'm not anymore.

And now we sit at dinner, and he talks to the kids about school and their activities while I watch them all quietly.

I study our son as he speaks to Mason in a formal, even tone, and wonder when he stopped being happy to share his excitement over things with his father. Dean is often animated and lively, and I feel as if I'm watching a robot, which makes my heart hurt even more.

And when he talks to Jenna, she's glum and short with him, refusing to speak to him as she stares down at her plate while moving the food around with her fork instead of eating it.

Even more confusing is that Mason ignores the way they're acting, keeping the smile on his face, and that's when I start to worry. And my concern grows when he suddenly tells the kids they can go to their friends for the weekend if they want. Both of their faces light up as the sudden urge to weep has me fighting to say nothing while keeping the tears at bay.

If he wants them gone, that means he wants to be alone with me, and it means I'm in trouble.

He excuses them from the table to go make plans and turns his focus to me. His eyes go from the softness he showed the children, to hard when they look at me as he stands up, pushing back his chair and tossing down his napkin before pointing at the table.

"Clean up." His demand is delivered with a nasty smirk. "I will take them to where they need to go. And when I return, you will be waiting for me upstairs."

Not trusting myself to speak, I simply nod at him, beginning to remove things from the table as he walks away without another word to me. I'm in the kitchen beginning to rinse off the dishes so I can stick them in the dishwasher, trying to keep my hands from shaking too much when Jenna and Dean come in to say goodbye.

"Love you," Dean says as I hug him and kiss the top of his head before he runs out the door.

Jenna's a little more reluctant, frowning at me as she pulls back from my hug. "You okay, Mom? You're not gonna be sick again, are you?"

"I hope not. I'm just a bit tired sweetie; that's all." As I turn back to the sink, refusing to meet her eyes, I keep my voice light as I tell her, "You have a good time, all right? I'll see you Sunday."

"Mom—"

"Let's go, Jenna." Mason cuts off whatever she was going to say as he walks into the kitchen, pointing to the door before I can ask where they are going. "I don't have all night."

Of course, she does as she's bid, whispering that she loves me before walking out the door.

Mason turns as he goes to walk out the door and gives me another hard look as he sweeps me from head to toe. "Be waiting for me, Leigh."

Then, he's gone, and I hurry to do the dishes with fear as my companion since he's deliberately getting rid of the kids for the weekend.

I don't know why. I haven't seen Cole since he told me who he is. I message him every day when I get a moment alone just to let him know I'm okay, but told him a few days ago we have to cool it after he asked when he could see me again.

Mason may not know why I lied to him when he assaulted me, but it's best to back off for a bit, especially with the way he's acting lately. I know something about my behavior tipped him off, made him think I needed to be put back in my place, and that's why he's acting like this.

I know he's mistreating me.

I don't stay because I'm stupid.

It's not because I don't want to leave. I do with everything in me. I know I should.

But it's not that simple.

He's not afraid to hurt me, he's shown that. He's not afraid of cutting back on his work at the office to do more at home and being around me so much I can't do anything, barely talk to anyone, or go anywhere. He's done it before. He even cut me off from speaking to my family, and when I disobeyed — even though I hadn't told them anything about what Mason did to me — he lied. He told them all sorts of nasty things about me, such as me having a little drug habit until they refused to talk to me anymore.

Plain and simple, it's dangerous. To leave him requires a strength I'm not sure I have, not when I know what I'm up against. Not when he could hurt me or the kids in his need to have us close; to have us as his. We're not people; we're not the family he loves and wants to protect. No, we're his possessions, and it's always been that way.

He doesn't care about Jenna or Dean's feelings, and he certainly doesn't care about mine. The fact he would openly flaunt his cheating by bringing the woman into our home proves that.

And yes, I'm terrified of taking such a huge step and its potential consequences for myself and the two people I love more than anything else in the world. Not to mention, as much as Cole wants to help me, asking him to put himself or his family at risk just doesn't sit right with me. The fact he's the step-son of Mason's boss is even worse. I wonder if he's told his family about us, and how I hadn't known all along.

A disheartening glimpse at my state of mind through the last nine years showing how I've failed on so many levels, especially considering the many times Mason had taken me to his boss' house. I'm sure that's only one detail of the many I apparently missed.

I had been too busy trying not to fuck up.

Stupid me, too, because I have to leave Mason, as I should've long ago. And I want to do it on my own; I want to free me and my children because it's the right thing, the thing a good mother does for her children when their father is a lying, manipulative, and abusive asshole.

I simply don't know how to do that without angering Mason to the point he does something reckless and dangerous; potentially to me and the children as well as himself, at that. Not that I care at this point. He would be doing me a favor by disappearing forever.

Finishing the dishes, I shut the water off, wipe off the counters and head upstairs to the bedroom. It's hard not to pace while waiting for him, so after a few moments, I go into my study and pull out the phone to send Cole a message.

"Mason sent kids to friends for the weekend. It's just me and him for the weekend so you may not hear from me. I'll text if I can."

My fingers strangle the phone, anticipating his reply because hearing from him makes me feel like everything is going to be okay, but all of my senses are on alert while dreading Mason's return.

He finally responds after two long minutes and tears well in my eyes at his reply. *"You know nothing good will come of this, babe."*

I know he's right, but not sure what else I can do

right now because I'm still working out how to leave. *"I'll be okay. I'll text you if I can."*

"He puts his hands on you, you do anything you can to call 911, Leighton. Got me?"

Taking a deep breath, I swipe at a runaway tear at the same time Mason's headlights turn into the driveway, tapping out a final text without responding to what he said or making any promises I can't keep. *"He's back. Gotta go."*

Deleting the texts real quick, I put the phone back in place and hurry back to the bedroom, sitting on the edge of the bed where he'll expect to find me. Hearing the garage door close once he's inside, his footsteps sounding in the hallway, and his footfalls on the steps as he heads this way makes my heart race and palms sweat. Wiping them on my jeans, I take a deep breath in hopes of calming the pounding in my chest so he won't notice how upset and anxious I am.

Impossible, though, as the moment he steps into the doorway glaring at me with cold eyes and a pinched mouth, my heart starts thumping hard enough it's noticeable even in my ears.

"Get undressed." His instruction is vicious, delivered with a rough slam of the door behind him, and the unnecessary yet chilling sound of the lock clicking. "Unless you'd like me to remove your clothing for you."

As I scramble off the bed, he must be satisfied with my reaction because he walks away to the master bath and shuts the door, allowing me to undress quickly. Before he returns, I put the clothes in the hamper he refers to as their 'proper place' once worn, so he can't yell at me for that.

Shutting its lid, I turn back toward the bed at the same time the door reopens. He emerges from the bathroom as nude as I am, making this moment the one where fear truly fills my heart.

But, it's the instant he moves until he's not even half a foot in front of me and opens his mouth when everything gets much worse. "I don't know who you're fucking behind my back, Leigh, but you'll stop all contact immediately. Understood?"

Mind reeling, wondering how he knows or how much he knows, I object without thinking. "I'm not fucking anyone—"

Even though I should've expected him to backhand me at any attempts to deny, the hit stings more than I thought it would. My right hand comes up to instinctively cover the spot he slapped as I fall back onto the bed.

"Don't fucking lie to me!" Roaring, he reaches out and yanks me back to my feet by my hair, his red face inches from mine as he enunciates every word. "You will stop immediately. You will tell him to leave you alone and not to contact you any longer. Do you fucking understand?"

"Yes." My response is a whimper, every part of me just wanting his painful grip on my hair to end enough to agree with anything. "Yes, I understand."

"You think I didn't notice you were slipping, Leigh? You know what I expect from you, don't you? You know your role in this household, and you were failing at it."

He's right. I haven't been trying hard enough to hide my feelings, and I don't care, but I say what he wants to hear. "I'm sorry—"

"I don't give a fuck." Malice drips from his words as he rattles his hand, sending pinpricks of pain through my scalp with the movement. "You honestly believe you'll leave here, leave me, ever? Go ahead and you'll never see your kids again. People may not like me, but they fear me. And I didn't spend all these years building up a reputation as loving husband and father for you to destroy it because you can't keep your fucking legs closed."

When I fail to respond, he grips my hair tighter and shakes me harder. It takes everything in me not to lift my hands toward his to try and remove them as he asserts, "You attempt to leave, you won't like the consequences. Do I make myself clear?"

The menace alone in that statement sends genuine terror straight to my brain and my heart because I know it's not an empty threat. And at this point, I'm not sure why the hell I've done this to myself since I knew the potential consequences if caught.

My reply comes out in a painful wail. "Yes."

Instantly, he lets go of my hair, but I don't stumble because he takes me in his arms like a lover would, and kisses the top of my head. "Good. I don't like being angry with you, and I won't be as long as you do what I say. You know that, don't you?"

"Yes, I do." Weak. I'm so weak.

"Of course you do." Using one hand, he lifts my chin until he's gazing down into my watery eyes and smirks at me. "I must be neglecting you if you felt the need to go outside our marriage, Leigh."

He pauses as if waiting for me to object, but after moments before, there isn't a chance in hell I'm saying a word. After a few tense seconds, he beams at me, the sudden change in demeanor throwing me off balance.

Every part of my body goes cold when he points at the bed. "Lay down in the center, Leigh, so I can give you the attention you were so desperate for that you went searching elsewhere."

When my response isn't instantaneous, his smile turns nasty, and he shoves me away from him hard. The angle causes me to drop down on the edge of the mattress, where I'm only able to catch myself by throwing my arms to the side, and clutching the comforter in my grip.

"Now," he snarls, glaring at me as I scramble to spin around and climb onto the bed, only to turn away after I'm lying in the center of the bed as directed.

Every second ticking by as he saunters around the room opening drawers increases my anxiety, my body trembling in response to the mix of cold air in the room and the dread in my heart.

Flipping the light off as he walks by the switch, the desire to get sick is something I have to force back as he gets into bed.

He climbs on top of me so his eyes stare right into

mine. "Hands above your head," he orders with an eerily sweet smile on his face.

Doing as he commands, he wraps a silky cloth around my wrists and slaps me in the face when I move my head to see what he's using. Cheek smarting, I force myself to look back at his face and focus on his nose. However, when he's finished tying my wrists, he makes it so I can't move by attaching what I assume is one of his ties to the headboard.

Holding my chin in the painful grip of his right hand, he cajoles in sweet, gentle tone that makes me want to vomit. "Tell me how much you want me, Leigh." His whole expression grows dark when I remain silent, squeezing on my chin until the pain moves up my jaw. "Say it."

Staring up into his face, I know that no matter what I do right now, he's going to have sex with me whether I say something or not. He's going to hurt me; he doesn't care what I want, and maybe it is stupid to invite pain, but I refuse to say what he wants me to say.

Instead, I lower my gaze and then to the side, which he swiftly punishes with an open-handed smack across my face. Releasing my chin, my ears ring as he snarls, "You will do as I say." He grabs my face again, eyes blazing with rage, spitting his demands. "Say it, Leigh."

Aware he'll make me regret it the moment I say what he wants me to, the only words out of my mouth are ones he pretends he doesn't want to hear, whispered due to his punishing grasp. "No, you son of a bitch."

"Have it your way," he rejoins with a laugh, moving

his hand to hold my nose closed until I'm forced to gasp for air, shoving what I quickly realize are a pair of my lace underwear in my mouth, choking me as his fingers jab the cloth into the back of my mouth.

With my body pinned under his, my kicks are automatic yet futile, and his chuckle is evil as he ties something around my face to keep them in my mouth. Then, he wraps one hand around my throat and gives a press firm enough to restrict my breathing.

"I've missed this," he informs me as I continue thrashing. Continuing to squeeze until my body stops moving, his actions make me fear I'll pass out. When I'm on the verge, he relaxes his grip enough my breaths through my nose are desperate while attempting to get enough air. "It's been a long time since you fought me; I forgot how much I enjoyed it."

He looks pleased as he says it; maybe it's the panic in my eyes or the desperate grabs for oxygen. I don't know.

Then, he puts his hand under my chin and tilts up, blocking my airways enough to restrict my breathing once more, and whispers, "Stay just like that." With his free hand, he lifts one of my legs around his hips and positions himself perfectly to intrude where he's not wanted.

This time, there's no hiding in my mind, safe in the arms of someone who cares for me in the way Mason doesn't, because he makes me keep my eyes open. He reminds me with every touch and kiss all over my body, every angry thrust of him inside me that I am his, forever and always. There's nowhere to run, no place to hide, where he won't make me pay for my transgressions.

I despise him. Hatred for him burns in my chest, the screams I don't dare let loose trapped in my chest even though the gag would muffle them; not that anyone would hear me, but I won't give him the satisfaction. Pure numbness spreads throughout my body, filling every limb, and wrapping around my heart in a way I never thought I would experience again.

A single tear gives away the despair I'm trying so hard to hide. Any fight left in me dies when he licks the tear up before it's able to slip off onto the pillow beneath my head. Chuckling as if it amuses him, he finishes inside me with one final painful thrust at the same time.

And when he finally removes himself from atop my body by rolling onto his side with a satisfied groan, I finally shut my eyes and let the darkness carry me away as it's been begging to do since he began.

16

"I'M FINE."

Three weeks have passed since that night with Mason, and every day since, Cole sends me a text asking if I'm okay. I give him the same answer every time, but we both know I'm not fine.

And I don't know if I ever will be again.

Not as if it matters.

"*No. You're not,*" he responds within seconds, making me panic as well as tear up when another arrives moments after. "*I know something's happened, babe. Don't treat me like I'm stupid.*"

I repeat what I've said so many times before, although my heart breaks every time I type it, fearing this will be the time he takes me seriously; the time he gives up on me. "*I told you it is over. Please. Just leave me alone.*"

Expecting him to respond as he always does by

telling me 'no,' he surprises me by countering with, "*Say that to my face. I won't believe you until then.*"

Of course, I can't. The moment his eyes land on me again, he'll know what Mason's done to me; what he's done every night since the first one. The proof isn't physical; no bruises, no hand prints, no marks of any kind because he's smarter than that. Rather than leave evidence as he had the night he lost control, this time the abuse is all emotional because sex between a husband and wife isn't noteworthy.

Especially after the first night where he took me unprepared. Now he's more careful to ease his entry by using something to help every time; so there's no physical way to confirm 'force' like he told me with a nasty laugh. And unlike when he used to make love to me, he tries to entice an orgasm from me as a way to show his power over me.

It hasn't happened.

It won't as long as I've got breath left in my body.

At least, that's what I tell myself, but I'm quickly learning that doesn't matter.

What Mason wants, Mason gets, and I've been stupid to forget it, to think there is any way out.

Devoid of nearly all emotion, I send Cole two final messages, forcing myself to type words that aren't true. "*I'm serious. Nothing's happened. He's not hurting me. We're over,*" is the first one, followed by, "*Turning this off, not turning it back on. Please leave me alone, Cole, if you care about me at all.*"

Not even waiting for the response he'll no doubt

make, I delete the thread with a whispered "forgive me" and turn off the phone, removing the battery.

Then, before Mason or the kids get home, I grab a hammer from the garage, letting all the anger and sorrow inside me explode in the extreme privacy of my fenced-in backyard. Smashing the phone over and over, until all its pieces resemble what letting Cole go has done to my heart.

EVENING ARRIVES, and for the first time in a while, Mason texts me from work saying he'll be late getting home.

It doesn't come without a warning, though.

He orders me to stay inside with the kids, order pizza, and watch a movie, and to wait for him as he prefers. Even though he says he'll be home at ten, which isn't too late, I'm grateful for the reprieve and the alone time with my children.

After I order the pizza, I head into the kitchen to get plates and napkins. When I turn to head back out, I discover Jenna standing silently in the entryway as Dean stomps up the steps behind her.

"Where's your brother going?"

She shrugs, taking a step toward me with a smile, and holds out her hands. "Let me carry those."

Caught off guard, and surely having misheard her, I blink a few times before asking, "What?"

Giggling, she snatches the plates from my hands, and

whirls around to leave again without replying. Her behavior is such a change from the last year, I'm not sure what to think, quickly following her into the living room. When she sets the plates down on the coffee table and takes a seat on the couch, I sit down to the left of her.

"Is everything okay, Jenna?"

Another bright smile from her, coupled with an intense vibe of peace from her worries me as she answers with, "Everything's perfect, Mom. Why?"

All my mom instincts scream at me, yet at the same time, her being happier is something I've hoped for many times now. Torn between two feelings, I try to turn the worried side into a joke. "You're not high, are you?"

She throws her head back and laughs before looking at me with twinkling eyes. "No, I'm not. Drugs are bad, right?"

When that's all she says, I'm left wondering if I should inquire further about her sudden change in attitude, or merely chalk it up to teenage hormones and let it go. The sound of Dean coming down the steps makes the decision for me, and part of me is relieved at having her in a good mood for once, so I drop the conversation completely.

Dean takes a seat to my left, leaving me in the middle between both of them, which works out well once the movie begins to play. Tears sting my eyes when I put an arm around each of them, and they snuggle into my side, something that hasn't happened in what feels like a lifetime. I'm almost depressed when the pizza arrives, and the snuggling ends, yet the laughter and general happiness of my children as we sit together eases some of my pain.

When it's twenty minutes before Mason's due to arrive home, all three of us make sure to wash the plates, straighten and clean the living room, before heading to get ready for bed. Once we reach the top of the steps, Dean hugs me before heading into the bathroom to brush his teeth, and Jenna ends up following me into my bedroom.

Not used to her trailing me around, it's hard not to smile when I turn to face her, and she's standing in front of the mirror on top of my dresser, pursing her lips in a rather exaggerated sort of way. Swiping my nightgown off the end of the bed, I walk over and give her shoulder a squeeze, hearing the bathroom door open at the same time.

"Your brother is done. You should head to bed as well, sweetie."

"Okay," she agrees easily.

Too easily.

As she walks away, my question is addressed toward her retreating form. "Are you sure you're all right, Jenna?"

Looking back over her shoulder as she reaches the doorway, she nods and beams at me as she says, "Yeah, I'm great actually. And you know I love you, right?"

"Of course, honey. I love you, too."

"I know. You're the best, Mom."

She's gone before I can say or do anything, and while

getting ready for bed, a small part of me remains unsettled and unnerved by her sudden cheerfulness. It's a gut feeling I'm unable to shake, even as I try to convince myself she's just a teenager. Teenagers are moody, especially girls, and no doubt she'll be back to her grumpy self by morning.

Once I've changed into my nightgown and brushed my teeth, I walk down the hall toward their rooms to make sure they are both in bed, and no lights are left on. Then, I head back to my room and climb into bed as the clock strikes ten, which has the added plus of allowing me to relax and fall asleep easily for the first time in a while.

THE SOUND of something crashing startles me awake with a gasp, a random sense of dread filling me while I glance around, confused about where the noise came from inside the house.

Mason lies beside me, turned away on his side and snoring, making me wonder if it had been my imagination. But when I hear a tortured moan coming from the direction of the kids' rooms, my movements are as gentle as can be to avoid waking Mason. I push the blankets off me, and take off at a gentle run once my feet touch the carpeted floor.

Seeing the light from Jenna's room shining through the tiny space at the bottom of her closed door, all my worries from earlier reappear. Mixed with new panic while arriving at the door to her room, I reach out to turn the handle slowly.

Both of my hands fly up to cover my gasp of shock at the sight of my daughter sprawled on the floor wearing nothing but a tank and underwear, lying unconscious in a puddle of her vomit.

Hurrying over to her, I kneel beside her and tap on her cheek, my words firm and urgent. "Jenna. Jenna. Wake up." When she doesn't respond to that, alarm and pure distress has me putting my hands on her shoulders and shaking her, raising my voice. "Jenna! Come on sweetie, wake up."

A sob rips from my chest as her eyes remain closed, the seriousness of what's going on finally sinking in as I take in her ashen face. Leaning down, I place my ear on her chest to listen for the sound of her heartbeat.

There, but just barely, her breathing shallow and fast.

Glancing up and around, I look around for a clue to what she's done as I stand up. Another sob breaks out at noticing an empty pill bottle on the other side of her body just under the bed.

That's when sheer anguish has me screaming Mason's name while running down the hall toward my room to grab the phone and call 9-1-1.

SIX OR SEVEN WEEKS PREGNANT.

The moment the doctor says the words about my thirteen-year-old daughter as we stand outside her room, the glare directed at him coupled with a vehement shake of my head. "That's impossible."

He speaks in a soft voice, his whole manner gentle, as if afraid I'll blow up at him any second. "I assure you it isn't, Mrs. Wright."

Lowering my body into the chair right next to the door, my sobs are difficult to hold back as they beg for a release. Putting my head in my hands with a moan, I ask him, "Did she… is the…?"

"Yes," he says with marked sympathy, understanding what I'm unable to finish asking as he takes a seat next to me.

After a second, he shows me her test results, explains that although it may have happened before she took the meds it's likely Jenna's overdose caused fetal death, and says how extremely lucky she is to be alive. He hands me papers to sign giving the staff my permission to give her a shot of some drug I can't even bother to pronounce right now that's meant to induce an abortion.

Reading the words, thinking about what's about to happen to my child, leaves a nasty taste in my mouth, and a gigantic ache in my heart. But I sign the papers because it's what needs to be done. He walks away after informing me they will administer it once she awakens, leaving me all alone with nothing but my thoughts for company.

Wrapping my jacket tight around my chest, I hate the fact I'm alone at this moment. Mason's home with Dean while our daughter's lying in a hospital bed having yet to awaken from her comatose state. I don't know what's worse: the fact my daughter ended up pregnant and I have no fucking idea who she would've had sex with, or the fact Mason instantly blamed me for the apparent fact our daughter tried to kill herself.

First, when and where was Jenna having sex? At school? The few times I let her go to the mall without me? Other than the time I caught her almost kissing Mark, I've never even heard of her having any interest in any boys at all.

And second, fuck Mason.

Fuck him for blaming me for our daughter trying to kill herself when he treats them like they don't exist except for when he needs to put on a show. Damn him for the way he treats me and threatens me, all while carrying on with his mistresses right in fucking front of me over and over through the years.

But mostly, I'm angry at myself because my daughter's been trying to get my attention, and instead of listening, I've been desperate to keep her in line while not walking the walk myself. She's been falling apart in front of my eyes, and I let her because I'm falling apart too.

It's my fault she's in that bed, and pregnant at thirteen, because she obviously sought affection and caring elsewhere like I had with Cole. The tight ache in my chest explodes, tears streaming down my cheeks at the thought of my daughter thinking I don't care; that I don't love her.

I do. I love her more than my life, and she should've known I would do anything for her.

It's obvious she doesn't know, though, and that's unacceptable.

Forgetting about myself, and shoving Mason's threats aside to worry about later, I do what I should've done for a while now.

Pulling the cell out of my pocket while taking a deep breath, I dial a number my heart memorized with blurry eyes and even shakier fingers.

I don't worry about him not knowing it's me because I gave him this number just in case. And I know it won't matter it's two a.m. to him, but when the phone rings once, twice, and then three times, doubt gives rise to fear there will be no answer. That I deserve to be ignored for what I've said, what I've done, and my failure to stay strong in the face of the monster who lies next to me in bed every night.

But then, there's a click, and Cole's deep voice, thick with drowsiness comes across the line. "Babe."

At the sound of his affection wrapped in that single word, I break completely. I give in to what I need, what my kids need, even if the admission goes against everything ever taught to me about being my own hero. I'm not brave like a hero, though; I'm a woman who needs help, whose children need help, and I admit it.

"I need you," I say through my whimpers, pushing the words past the lump in my throat and the anxiety rolling over me. "I don't want to need you, but I—I can't do this on my own. I thought I could—"

"Babe," he cuts in among my babbling, his voice a little stronger now as he clears his throat, tone growing firm and assertive by the second. "I know why you did that earlier, but you say the word, Leighton. I'll come and take you away from there. All three of you."

Crying harder from sadness mixed with the reassurance of his presence in my life, all I can manage to breathe out is, "Cole…"

"That's it," he huffs when I say nothing else. "I'm coming right now, and I'm bringing the cops with me."

"God no." Taking a deep breath in, I let it out slowly, swiping at my wet cheeks with my free hand. "Jenna's in the hospital, Cole. She…she tried to kill herself. And I'm here w-waiting for her to… wake up."

For a moment, there's complete silence.

Then, his straightforward and gentle declaration. "I'm on my way."

Click.

And at the same moment I slip the phone back in my pocket, Jenna's ear-piercing and agony filled screams announce her return to consciousness.

17

BEEP...BEEP...BEEP.

Dragging my eyes open at the annoying noise, it takes me a few seconds to realize I've fallen asleep in the chair across from Jenna's emergency room bed. Jolting up, the nurse standing next to the bed chuckles softly and says, "Just checking on your daughter. Sorry to wake you."

"It's all right."

She takes a step away from the bed and turns to me with a smile. "A man arrived earlier for you, but he wasn't allowed back here since he said he wasn't family and we didn't have your permission. I believe he said he'd be waiting for you in the lobby."

Cole.

"Damn." Looking around for a clock, the time shows it's been two hours since I called him, and I must've dozed off after they'd calmed Jenna down and she'd fallen back asleep. Unwilling to leave Jenna's side, I return my eyes back to the nurse and ask, "His name is Cole Vaughn. Will you please see if he's still out there and let him in if he is? He's a family friend."

"Absolutely." She flicks her gaze at Jenna with a soft smile. "I wouldn't want to leave my daughter either. If you need anything else, just let me know. I'll be at the nurse's desk."

At my nod, she leaves the room and after what feels like forever, the curtain protecting anyone from peering in through the glass doors is shoved aside as Cole steps inside.

I don't even take a breath before flying into his arms, which he encircles around my body to hold me tight, my tears rushing forth as if I hadn't cried buckets earlier already. It doesn't last long though, especially not when the tears subside and everything that's gone on surges to the forefront of my mind, causing me to stiffen in his grasp.

He drops his arms even as his question is filled with confusion. "Babe?"

"Don't me call me that here." I step away enough we're not touching while also being able to look him in the face. When he stares at me and doesn't respond with anything more than a lift of his right brow, I grab a tissue from near the sink, blowing my nose before throwing it away and snatching a fresh one. Taking a seat back in the chair, I keep my eyes focused on Jenna while addressing him. "Have you been waiting long?"

"Since about twenty minutes after you called me, yes."

"I'm sorry. You didn't have to—"

"Yes, I did." He cuts me off and then lets out a heavy sigh. "You called me, I told you I would be here. I wasn't leaving until you said otherwise."

I want to thank him for coming, but all I feel is guilty for having him here; for needing him here even. It's hard not to look at him, yet I know if I look at him, everything I feel and have been going through will be written all over my face.

He's going to see it and know, I'm sure. Any second he's going to make me lift my gaze and meet his, and it's going to be over. He'll go after Mason, and that's what I don't want, no matter what he's done to me. He can't be here for me if he's in jail, justified or not in his actions.

However, he doesn't do as I believe. Instead, he steps closer to the bed and asks in a soft tone, "What happened?"

My response is flat, wobbling on the edge of tears once more, as I lower my eyes to the floor in front of me. "She took her whole bottle of sleeping pills. She's lucky she got sick and that I found her when I did."

"She is. Do you know why she did it?"

I assume he's asking if she left a note, but I honestly don't know because I hadn't even considered it. All my efforts had focused on getting her to the ER, but the way she acted before going to bed makes me say, "I think she said goodbye to me earlier in the evening without me realizing it at the time. No need to leave a note."

A silent pause, and then I feel him kneel in front of

me, putting his hands on my knees even though my head remains bowed.

"Why," he whispers close to my ear, "do I get the feeling you aren't saying something else? Something important?"

The desire to confide in him and share the reality of the situation is impossible to ignore. That's why I called him, isn't it? I have to trust someone, hand over my power, having faith he won't abuse it so my children and I can get out of our current environment. I need his strength in a time when mine just isn't enough to do what needs done.

"She is…" Sucking in a deep breath, I let it out bit by bit before slowly lifting my head to meet his gentle gaze with my teary one. "She was pregnant."

A whole world of emotions skip over his face, from shock to disbelief to grief, his eyes closing briefly as he swallows hard before he opens them back up to stare at me. "Was?"

"Six or seven weeks," I confirm with a nod, sitting back while crossing my arms over my chest, and glancing away. "They can't be sure her suicide attempt was the cause, but it's likely. She may have known, which may be why…but I…I didn't know."

"Of course you didn't. How could you?"

"I should, shouldn't I? She's thirteen. I don't even know who she would've gotten pregnant by, or where—"

"Hey. Look at me." He waits until I'm looking at him as requested, his smile tender as his hands squeeze my knees in reassurance. "Teenagers are pretty inventive and will find a way to do something if they want to bad enough. As for boys, she's only in my class for thirty minutes twice a week, but I've never seen her speak with any of them."

"What about Mark?"

"That boy you told me trying to kiss her at the mall?" At my nod, he says with a thoughtful expression, "Honestly, I'm not sure that kid's even hit puberty yet."

Not sure whether he's serious or not, it's the quirk of his lips and the crinkling at the corners of his eyes which lets me know he's joking. And even though nothing about this situation is funny, I have to cover my mouth in order to smother my sudden laughter. Of course, it's that exact amusement which turns into sobs at the hopelessness I feel and when Cole gathers me in his arms once again, I wrap mine around his neck and lets myself fall apart for the first time in a long while.

AT EIGHT IN THE MORNING, Cole sits next to me in the chair a nurse brought in for him about an hour after he joined me earlier. His hand holds mine, our fingers interlaced, and except for when either of us go to use the bathroom, he refuses to let go.

I've spent the whole night alternating between fear and bliss, hope and doubt, even with his reassurance everything will be fine. It's a beautiful thought, but life has taught me otherwise since I'm far from anywhere near fine.

"I knew it."

The sound of Jenna's voice, soft and scratchy, causes me to jump out of my chair and drop Cole's hand as if it burns, but it's too late. The way she's partially sitting up gives her a perfect view of our chairs, and therefore, our handholding.

"Hi, Mom," she says when my eyes land on her pale face and blinding smile. "Hi, Mister Vaughn."

"Jenna." He stands up. "I will leave while you two talk."

"Don't go," she pleads with him while continuing to keep her gaze focused on me. "Mom needs you."

With a soft chuckle, he says, "Your mother needs to talk to you. In the meantime, I'll go see what they've got for breakfast."

He strides out of the room, leaving us alone, and that's when Jenna breaks her focus on me to stare down at her now clasped hands.

"Where's Dad?"

Her question is a mumble, and after walking to her side, I rest my hand on her shoulder. "He's at home with Dean."

"Did he even care?"

I'm left at a loss for words, because I can't tell her the accusations her father threw at me, or the way he really hadn't been concerned about whether his daughter would make it or not. His absence answers her question all on its own, and when she glances back up at me staring down at her while trying to formulate a response, she frowns but doesn't say anything more.

There are so many questions she needs to answer, but the one I want to know the most is what finally emerges. "Why, Jenna?"

"Why what?"

"You could've died." Her lack of response and the accompanying shrug frustrates me to the point I snap at her without thinking, all my pain from the last twelve hours erupting. "Do you have any idea how you made *me* feel? Don't you think I fucking care? I'm your mother and I love you and you did that knowing I would find you!"

Her eyes shimmer with tears as her hands lift out of her lap, unclasping as they inch closer to her face, and her whole countenance collapses with misery. "I'm sorry," she whispers, tears spilling over and running down her cheeks. "I didn't know what else to do."

Softening my tone, and not sure if she knows about the pregnancy or not, I ask her gently, "About what? Nothing is so big we can't find a solution for it, Jenna. You should've trusted me with whatever it is."

"I can't." Her shoulders shake as she covers her mouth with her hands, wailing into them while I stand beside her feeling helpless and needing to tell her what has happened to her pregnancy.

Dropping down the arm of the bed, I wrap my arms around her and draw her toward me. When she clings to me like she hasn't done since she was a toddler, I decide to wait on asking her anything else. What's most important is giving her the comfort she so desperately needs right now even if I don't understand what led her here in the first place.

TWO IN THE afternoon and Mason still hasn't come to see Jenna at the hospital. Instead, thirty minutes ago he sent me a text message asking when they would release her, the time we'll be home, and what I'm making for dinner.

Asshole.

I sent him a message telling him I'm not sure she's coming home tonight and to order a pizza. I haven't heard from him since but I know once I return to the house, he'll berate me for not being able to do what he wanted me to.

Good thing I don't plan on staying longer than to get mine and the kids' things so we can move the hell out.

"Don't worry about her." Cole clasps my hand a bit tighter as he interrupts my thoughts. "Psych evaluations are standard for attempted suicides."

"I know."

We're sitting outside her room while she's inside with the doctor sent to evaluate her. Although I could've chosen to stay in the room with her, I thought she might be more open about why she tried to kill herself if I weren't in the room, especially since she apparently had no clue about being pregnant.

However, after being informed of that and the follow-up care required, she remained calm and allowed them to give her the shot without saying anything at all. When I asked her if she was upset or needed to talk, she'd simply said with zero emotion, "I didn't even know," and turned over on her side to take a nap.

Logically, I know right now, especially at her age, everything that's happened has yet to hit her. It will, and no matter when or how it does, there's no doubt I'll be there to help her get through it in a way I haven't been in a long time.

When the door to her room finally opens, Cole lets go of my hand, and we both stand up as the doctor shuts it softly behind him. Clearing his throat, he regards me with sad eyes that set off my anxiety and then glances at Cole.

"I'll need to speak with Mrs. Wright in private."

"No. He can stay. Just tell me what she said."

"Mrs. Wright, there is some sensitive information which should only be discussed with you and her father—"

"Do you see her father here?" Lifting my hands with palms up, I look to my left and right before dropping my hands and taking Cole's in mine, interlacing our fingers while glaring at the doctor. "I'm just going to tell him anyway, so please spare me the time and effort, and tell me what's going on."

When he drops his gaze to our hands and lifts his gaze back up to simply stare without speaking and clear judgment in his expression, Cole says, "It's all right, Leighton—"

"No." Tossing a quick frown at him, I address the

doctor once more, this time in a lowered and irritated voice. "Listen to me. My daughter has been through enough, as have I, and if her father gave two fucks about her or what's going on, he would be here wouldn't he? So stop it with your judgmental attitude and looks about something you know nothing about, and tell me why my daughter tried to kill herself. If you know, that is."

"I do." He responds with wide eyes, shuffling his feet while lowering his focus to the clipboard and the papers attached to it, before lifting two fingers to pinch the bridge of his nose as he gives into my reprimand. "In my discussion with Jenna, it appears as if the attempt was for attention. However, she wasn't seeking yours, but that of a male she refuses to refer to as anything other than 'he.' No matter which way I attempted to extract more information about him, she withheld any further details other than to say the sex between them was consensual."

My mind reels at the idea my daughter's been hiding a relationship, and even if she said she was in on it, she's not old enough to consent to sex with anyone. Attempting to keep from freaking out, I grasp onto his last sentence containing a word popping up for the second time today. "Was?"

This is where his sad looks graduate to straight up tortured. "Yes. According to Jenna's timeline of events, the last time they slept together would've been around the estimated date of conception. She stated, and I quote, 'We had sex and after, he told me we can't see each other anymore. I told him I loved him and he said that's nice, but it didn't change how he felt. He didn't even care about me crying or anything.' End quote."

Feeling faint at hearing how callously Jenna was treated, I lower myself into the chair while Cole sits in the one beside me and growls, "Fucking dick."

No wonder she didn't want to tell me. She must've known the doctor would tell me what she said in the room, yet I understand why she would rather someone else did it for her. I would've asked her the million questions I have, such as who, when, and how long this has been going on.

On that thought, I ask him, "What's the estimated date?"

For a second he looks confused, then he clears his throat and says, "Six or seven weeks would have conception around the end of September."

Instantly, I know what day it was: the day I found Jenna in the bathroom crying. Deciding I'll share with Cole later, I keep my face neutral as I nod at the doctor. "Thank you. Is there anything else I should know?"

He turns the clipboard toward me and holds out the pen as he shakes his head. "Other than your signature, and a recommendation for your daughter to continue her sessions with her psychiatrist and obtain therapy, I've come to the conclusion your daughter isn't a threat to herself or others. From her responses, her actions were an impulse and done out of desperation, not a true desire to end her life. However, I suggest you meet with her psychiatrist as soon as possible and discuss her medication regimen."

Signing where he indicates, I hand everything back to him and say, "I will definitely do that. Thank you."

When he walks away, I don't even last a few seconds before I'm crying for what seems like the thousandth time today, wondering how everything got this messed up.

And blaming myself for all of it.

18

"HELLO, MRS. WHITFIELD."

Cole's mother, with her wavy black hair and green eyes so like his making me feel ridiculous at not having realized she's his mother, greets me with a gentle smile as she steps back from the doorway. "Please, Leighton. Call me Nell. Come inside out of that cold, all three of you."

Dean stalks past her carrying his book bag and suitcase filled with clothes, asking her in the exuberant manner of his I've missed and am so glad to see again, "Do I get to call you Nell, too?"

"I don't know young man," she replies with a chuckle and a wink at me. "How do you typically address your elders?"

Jenna steps inside, her head bowed and holding her bag in front of her, not speaking as I follow her over the threshold enough Nell is able to close the door and Dean sighs.

"Mister or Missus and their last name."

If I weren't so exhausted from the past few days, I would laugh at the slight scorn in his voice, but Nell doesn't seem bothered by it as she laughs again.

"I think we should stick with what's proper, don't you? Wouldn't want you to forget your manners when it really counts." She turns to me, nodding at the door to my left while addressing all of us. "Now, while your mother waits for me in the living room, why don't I show you two to your rooms and you can put away your things before dinner. Follow me this way, please."

Both of them walk away with her, but only Dean tosses me a smile over his shoulder. Jenna hasn't spoken to me since the day she talked with the doctor eleven days ago. They released her the following afternoon, and upon returning home, she's done nothing except hide in her room while ignoring everyone.

Cole tried to talk me out of going home completely, but once I told him my plan, he had relaxed a little even if his worry became quite evident. He went his way with marked reluctance while I went mine, and once home I kept my head down and mouth shut around Mason.

Then today, on the day before Thanksgiving, he left for work at eight a.m. and sent me a text message at noon saying he would be home at six so I better have dinner ready.

Only, if he arrives home for dinner in the next ten minutes as he said he would, he'll be shocked to find me and the children gone, along with some of our things. He'll try to call me but my phone will ring from where it sits on the dining room table, and the day after tomorrow, he'll be served with divorce papers drawn up by a lawyer courtesy of the Whitfield's.

Other than the essentials such as clothing, our passports and any important papers like birth certificates, I took nothing else from the house. Although I'm entitled to many things, in the end all I care about is getting away from him, and I don't care if it means I end up with nothing from the life we shared together.

When I shut the front door behind me earlier, there had been no sadness, no caring at all. The relief I felt at walking away and getting into a taxi with my kids has turned into a peace I haven't experienced in over a decade. The fact neither questioned my decision to have them pack their things because I was leaving their father said more than any words could convey; witnessing the difference my decision's already made in Dean's demeanor solidifies the fact I've made the right choice.

Finally.

At the sound of a car door closing, I head into the living room after realizing I'm still standing right in the middle of the foyer and take a seat on the couch just as the front door opens. Male laughter, loud and happy, followed by someone running past the living room entryway, and then Cole shouting, "Not chasing you bro, so you better give those back right fucking now."

"No way!"

"You crush them, and I'll crush you—"

"Bring it. I've been going to the gym."

Trying not to chuckle at their back and forth, I'm unable to hold it in any longer when Cole retorts,

"Really? Is that why you're starting to resemble a bobble head? All that hot air."

Busting into full out laughter, not even two seconds pass before Cole's strides into the room with an enormous grin on his face and stops less than a foot from where I sit. Slipping his hands into his pockets, he winks at me as my snickering subsides. "Hey, babe."

"Hey."

"Why are you in here all alone?"

"Your mother took Dean and Jenna upstairs—"

I don't get to finish my sentence because my mouth drops open as something smacks into the back of Cole's head.

He whirls around, expression filled with disbelief. "You fucker! You ruined them."

Dropping my gaze to the floor, I see what was apparently a bouquet of flowers now strewn all over the place, and looking over to the doorway reveals the culprit.

"Jack." I greet his brother with a laugh, rising and stepping up beside Cole for a better view as my feet crush the flowers beneath them. "It's been a while."

"Mizz Wright." His exaggerated drawl amuses me even though I see Cole roll his eyes out of the corner of my own at his brother's antics. "I didn't know you were here, and I think those flowers were for you. Whoops."

"No, you ass, they were for Mom."

Jack, with his shaved head and always twinkling blue eyes, puts a hand over his gaping mouth in a mocking gesture, speaking through his fingers. "You didn't get your girlfriend flowers? See, this is why I'm married and you aren't. You can't romance your way out of a wet paper bag."

Shocked by his words, my head jerks back as I blink rapidly, holding up a hand with my palm out while gaping at him. "Wait. What? Aren't you like twenty?"

"Just turned, actually," he confirms with a nod, his face beaming with happiness. "Married Laurie 'bout a month after we graduated from high school. Her parents weren't happy, but we don't care. We've been together since fifth grade, what did they think we had to wait for?"

"Two weirdos in a pod," Cole comments while nudging me in the side with a chuckle. "She's great, you'll like her."

My response to him is delivered with a smile and raised brows. "I've met her, at the get-togethers. You know, the ones you didn't attend?" As he mock glares at me, I turn my focus back on Jack, telling him, "Congrats, by the way. And sorry I missed it. I've always liked Laurie."

"Thanks. It wasn't anything big anyway; just family. And she'll be here tomorrow so you can see her then." Looking down at his watch, he straightens from where he's leaning against the frame, and sighs. "And on that note, gotta go. Dinner with her family today and she'll murder me if I'm late. Women!"

He leaves without a backward glance and Cole sighs before crouching down after a few moments. "Probably should clean these up before mom arrives and pitches a fit about how I'm always ruining her carpets."

As I bend down to help him, his mother's amused tone rings out from the doorway. "Too late, but I heard most of your and Jack's shenanigans from upstairs."

Grabbing the last of the petals, Cole stands and walks over to the little wastebasket by the side table, and drops them inside as I do the same. "He destroyed your flowers."

"No big deal. After all, it's the thought that counts, so thank you, honey." After a gentle smile at him, she steps closer until she's right in front of me and takes my hands in hers. "How are you?"

"I haven't felt as good as I do right now in a long time, Mrs—I mean, Nell. Thank you so much for your help with everything, and for letting us stay here. I promise it won't be long—"

"Oh, no need for any of that and it's truly our pleasure." She squeezes my hands a little before letting go. "You three are welcome to stay as long as necessary, and I mean that. No need to rush at all."

She's always been kind to me, and this is no exception, yet my eyes still get watery at her generous and sincere offer of her home as a safe haven. It makes my heart ache knowing I could've trusted them all those years ago to help me if I would've just reached out after the day in the parking lot.

"I wish I would've done it sooner," I admit in a small, tired voice that's unable to hide the despair I've kept bottled up so long. "And it's difficult to believe it's real."

"Well, it is." Cole steps closer to me and starts to slip his hand around my waist, but removes it the instant he feels me stiffen. The resulting grind of his teeth makes my heart ache even more because it's not his touch I fear and it's plain he knows because his words remain tender and affectionate. "Come on, let me show you where your room is and then we'll all eat."

I see his mother's eyes flick from me to him and back, the smile never leaving her face, yet for the umpteenth time I wonder if she's aware of the relationship between us even though it's obvious Cole at least told Jack. But then as she turns to leave the room to check on dinner, I wonder why it matters, or if it even does at all.

When Cole slips his hand into mine — the only kind of touch beyond the hugs at the hospital he's been able to do without me flinching — I realize I don't care if anyone likes it or not. And not because I'm ungrateful for her help, but the fact I'm here as a direct result of her son's influence in my life. Plus, I've cared for too long about what someone thought of the things I did, and look where that's gotten me until now.

He grabs my suitcase, leading us out of the room and up the steps, taking a right at the top of them. Then, stopping at the last door in the long hallway, he lets go of my hand and opens the door, letting me walk through first.

Setting my suitcase by the dresser as I turn and face him, he leans against the doorframe and watches me without saying anything. Although things were okay downstairs, the fact he keeps so much distance between us now makes me feel awkward, even though I'm aware he's giving me space because he knows something bad happened.

I haven't told him what Mason did. I don't know how to begin or even where to begin. And now that I'm safely in this beautiful room with it's four poster bed, creme colored walls, and the matching carpet not even twenty minutes away from where I've been living, reality catches up with me.

Relief at my freedom, fear it won't last, and the things Mason might do to me if he gets his hands on me cause my chest to tighten painfully. Both of my hands come up to cover my heart as it starts to beat a wild pace through my chest, so hard it feels like my ears pulse with the pressure, and Cole's alert in an instant, straightening off the wall.

"Something wrong?"

Closing my eyes in what feels like slow motion, I blow out a steady breath. "Come in and shut the door."

Doing as I bid with a soft click, he takes a few steps closer before halting once more, guessing what I'm about to do. "Tell me."

"First you promise me," I whisper with a pointed glance down at his hands balling into fists. "Unless he tries to hurt me again, he's not worth it, okay? He's not worth the trouble."

He nods, locking his gaze with mine as the tick in his jaw gives away his building ire at the information he knows is about to come his way. "You and the safety of Jenna and Dean are all I care about, babe."

"Good." Moving to the edge of the bed, I sit on it and look down at my clasped hands while starting from the morning I found out who he was.

Every word is forced past my lips, bringing him closer and closer to me until he's sitting next to me, and covering my hands with one of his.

By the end, when tears are streaming down my cheeks even though the weight of what I've been keeping from him is lifted, turning toward him to see his reaction is all that's left. And I'm not prepared to find him staring at me with watery, red eyes and an intense expression, or for what he says next.

He lifts his right hand to my face, cupping my cheek in his hand, and leans in to press a gentle kiss on my lips before saying barely an inch away from them, "You are the strongest and most resilient woman I've ever met in my life, babe, and I'm so proud of you for realizing you needed to get away no matter how scared you are."

Swiping a tear that slips down my cheek, I take a deep breath and admit, "I'm still afraid."

"I know, and I want to beat the fucking shit out of him for what he did, but I won't. I'm here for you and I won't let you down. I'll help you."

The pad of his thumb strokes my cheek, while his heated breath warms my lips with the promises delivered from his mouth, and the desire for him to hold me wars with my new fear of being touched.

However, this is Cole, and somehow he knows what I

need without me even saying it. He moves away from me, pulling off his shoes before climbing onto the bed and resting against the pillows. He opens his arms, leaving whether or not I get close to him as my decision to make, and after some hesitation, I mimic his actions and let him hold me in a loose embrace.

The feel of him pressing a kiss against the top of my head is the last thing I remember before falling asleep not even a few minutes later as the toll of these difficult weeks catches up to me.

19

SITTING at the table with Cole's family doesn't compare to any holiday dinner I've ever experienced.

As always, his family is loud. We're all crammed around the dining room table, which is pretty big compared to any I've ever sat at, but still not enough to fit all of us comfortably. However, nobody seems to care, because everyone is laughing, cracking jokes, and talking over one another in general.

Well, except Jenna, who had simply grabbed a plate and gone back to her room, with both Nell and my own's permission. I wish she would've stayed down here and joined in, but forcing things is her father's way, not mine. It's also not even been a week since her suicide attempt, and with Nell's assistance, I'm still working out how to best help my daughter while also trying to figure out who the hell she'd slept with.

Her depression has piled on top of my sadness, but

unlike her, I refuse to wallow in it when I'm free for the first time since Mason put his ring on my finger.

So I'm happy to sit here at the table with the Whitfield's and enjoying myself immensely, with Dean to my left and Cole to my right. Across from us is Laurie and Jack, with both his sisters — eighteen-year-old sister Zoe and sixteen-year-old Rose — to his left. Nell's at one end while Mister Whitfield is at the other; using his first name is something I think I'll have trouble with for a while due to him being Mason's boss all these years.

And honestly, it's a little strange that Cole has a sister who is only three years older than Jenna, but I suppose I'm the only one even a little bothered by it.

"So, Leighton," Nell says, gaining my attention with the statement and smiling at me when I look her way while everyone stops talking as she claps her hands. "You should know that we have a tradition of gift giving for Thanksgiving since, at Christmas time, we serve others through various means and don't exchange presents."

"You do?" I get the quite obvious hint that I'm among the recipients of said presents, and immediately attempt to turn them down graciously. "That's sweet, but you've done so much already—"

"Don't try to tell mom no," Cole interrupts with a laugh, snatching my hand up from my lap and giving it a squeeze. "She won't listen no matter how much you protest."

Nell laughs, scooting back her chair while standing, and looks straight at Cole. "That's correct. Now, come and help me, since you were all in on it."

He leans in and pecks my cheek before standing, laughing at me when I aim a small glare his way. Jack also gets up and follows them, while his sisters start to clear the table, assuring both me and Laurie they don't need any assistance when we offer to help. Mr. Whitfield merely continues eating his food, winking at me when I glance at him, and I wonder how such a happy man put up with my husband as his employee for as long as he has.

"Awesome!" Dean claps his hands beside me, eyes wide with excitement when I finally move my focus to him. "I wonder what they got us!"

So do I, especially when they all come back into the room carrying individual piles of presents, and set them in the center of the now cleared off table.

The gifts are separated and placed in front of each of us; I notice we each have five. Cole sits back down and leans over to whisper in my ear, "Jenna's presents were put aside. You can take them up to her later."

"Thank you." Nodding at my boxes I ask him, "Which one is from you?"

"This one." He rearranges my boxes, placing a decent sized rectangular one in front of me even as he says, "This is one of two. But you'll have to wait for the other."

Eyeing the simple white bow on the box, I pick it up and smile sheepishly at him while turning it over. "This isn't fair. I didn't get you anything."

"I consider you being here my present." With a blush, I shake the box and pout when it doesn't make any noise, slipping my finger underneath the tape to unwrap it. At the sight of a box that holds a shiny new smartphone in it, I lift my gaze to his and find him watching me with a smirk. "Let's not beat this one to pieces with a hammer, all right?"

I want to cry, but with tears of happiness rather than sadness. "Thank you. But—"

"Ah-ah." He holds up a finger and wiggles it, chuckling as he answers my question before I can ask it. "You're welcome. And in case you're wondering, the phone was my idea, but it's actually through dad's business, and it's unlimited. All of our numbers are already in it, and we all have your number; the phone is completely ready to use."

Before I can respond to that, Dean tugs hard on my arm, and he's beaming when I turn to find him holding up a box with a phone as well. "Look Mom! My own phone!"

Keeping my eyes from widening at him having a phone at his age, Nell pipes up with a soft explanation. "He needs one. Jenna needs one. You all need one, just in case. Their phones are limited, though; calls and texts to you, each other, David and I, plus Jack and Cole. And of course, emergency numbers. That's it."

Acknowledging the limits are exactly what I would've done, I don't know how to respond, and give her a gracious smile when she reaches over and picks up a small, flat square box.

"Open this one next," she says, holding it out for me

to take and placing it in my palm when I extend my hand.

It's not hard to open, and tears genuinely threaten to fall when I pull out a key that obviously goes to a car, and my mouth drops open. "Nell…"

Both Cole and her laugh as she says, "Don't get too excited or upset about it. This goes to a company car which was recently put out of commission. However, it's still in good condition, and we saved it just for you."

"Saved it…?"

Cole and Nell exchange a look, but before I can ask what for Mr. Whitfield's phone blares loudly from the other end.

"Shit," he curses, his mouth flattening in a grim line as he picks up his phone and answers it while the whole table falls into silence as if commanded to hush. "Mister Wright."

My stomach drops, sucking in a breath when he brings his sympathetic gaze to mine and uses his other hand to wave in a dismissive fashion. When his two girls stand, I realize he's sending out the children, and turn to Dean only to find him already grabbing his things and rising as well with the assistance of Nell.

She walks them out, Cole reaching over and taking my hand in his, interlacing our fingers while I focus on his dad once again.

"I'm sorry to hear that."

It's interesting to listen to what he says, only to watch his free hand curl into a fist as he lowers it to the table, his face growing more stormy by the second at whatever Mason is saying. And even though he doesn't know I'm here, safely hidden behind the walls of their house, my heart beats so hard I fear Cole can feel it through where we touch.

"I'm sure your wife is fine, Mister Wright. Did she have a vacation planned that you may have forgotten about?" He pauses, listening even as his mouth turns down into a frown. "I see. I'm sorry, but I can't spare you from the office tomorrow due to the holidays and lack of staff." Another few moments of silence from him as he listens to whatever Mason is saying, the corner of his mouth quirking up again when he finally speaks. "Yes, I'll see you at the office tomorrow. Good night."

The moment he hangs up, Jack snarls, "That fucking asshole. Calling you, of all people. Think he knows?"

"After all this time? No, although he seemed suspicious."

"He might know," I admit softly, remembering him telling me to cut off contact with whoever I was sleeping with. "He knew I was seeing someone, but I don't know if he knew who it was."

Cole clutches my hand tighter as his gaze locks on mine. "He'll know tomorrow when he receives the divorce papers. He's a long time employee; he'll recognize the lawyer's name. It won't take him long to put it all together if he hasn't already."

Nell's voice rings out as she walks back into the dining room and slides back into her seat. "Good. It's about time. Personally, I look forward to the day you fire his ass, darling."

And it's the moment she says that when everything truly hits me. The car, the phones, the immediate acceptance into their house, the way they are on pins and needles to fire Mason; all of it clicks into place.

"You all planned this." The words are accusatory, angry even though I know they would've needed to plan somewhat to help me, and I jerk my hand out of Cole's as I focus my glare on him. "Tell me what the hell's going on."

"Missus—Leighton," Mister Whitfield says in a firm voice, waiting until I lift my eyes to meet his, which are soft and understanding. "A man with a bad temper, an abusive past, and no job to occupy him is a dangerous individual. I would've fired your husband many years ago if I hadn't worried he would move away to where we wouldn't be able to protect you or your children."

"So what, you've been waiting years? For me?" When he just looks at me and gives a curt nod, I shove back my chair to stand. Slapping my hands down on the table in the first free display of anger I've been allowed to have in a long time, tears pool in my eyes and blur my vision as I glare at everyone of them. "All this time, all these years... I was alone and felt trapped and helpless, and you guys knew all along?"

I feel Nell's hand cover my left one, her voice wobbly with emotion when she speaks. "I'm sorry you felt alone. You were never alone. We watched out for you the best we could without him being able to catch on."

Blown away by all of this information, I don't know where to look or turn, choosing to pull my hand out from underneath Nell's and walk over to a window as she continues talking to my back.

"Much as we wanted you to leave, you didn't seem open to leaving on your own. When Cole told us you two began something, we both highly disapproved. Not of your relationship, but because Mason is not a man we want to take chances with. We've watched for signs because if we absolutely had to push it, we would've approached you, but it's clear he wasn't abusing you as he was before."

Her last statement doesn't seem like a question, yet I find myself answering it anyway as other fears take hold and refuse to go away. "He… hadn't been physical in a long time, except in an attempt to intimidate me by backing me into a corner, up until a few weeks ago."

"Yes, Cole told us about that, and we started to plan accordingly. We wanted to make sure you knew you had a way out if you wanted or needed it."

Facing them again, I look right at Cole, my voice rising by the second. "And what if we hadn't begun something? You never would've known." My hands ball at my sides as unexpected embarrassment and anger completely take over. "Did you do it deliberately? Was fucking me just a way to get me out of there?"

Cole blanches, the sound of everyone else's shock barely registering in my mind as he stares at me for a moment before finally answering with a shake of his head and a hand shoved through his hair. "You ran into me, Leighton. I merely took a chance on the attraction between us."

Instead of replying to him with every one of my doubts, I glance at Mister Whitfield, then at Nell and say, "I had no idea he was your son. Not until the day he showed up at my house. That's how out of it I've been for so long. No fucking idea. And now to know all these years you've been keeping an eye on me…I…I need to be alone."

Running from the room, I head toward the room they've put me in, barely making it inside before I burst into tears. The doubt which had started creeping in downstairs releases full force, causing me to wonder if not only had all the years with Mason been a lie, but the moments I've had with Cole since I met him as well.

The fact I don't know makes me cry even harder, until I can no longer keep my eyes open, and I manage to crawl into bed, feeling the loneliest I've ever felt in my life as sleep claims me.

20

THE SOUND of a soft knock at the door, followed by it creeping open slow and unsure before gently closing, wakes me up the next morning.

Rubbing at my burning eyes, a few rapid blinks make it easier for me to see in the brightness of the day, and I turn over just as the gentle sound of Cole's voice announces his presence.

"Sorry, Leighton," he says when my eyes locate him standing not far inside the door. "Didn't mean to wake you."

"Oh. It's okay. I probably should get up anyway."

"Don't do that."

Yawning, I cover my mouth with my hand, letting it all out before asking, "Do what?"

"Say something is okay if it isn't."

"You knocked and came in, anyway." It's hard not to keep the amusement out of my voice as he strides toward me. "If you didn't mean to wake me, why would you knock?"

He stops by the side of the bed and frowns. "I wanted to check on you. I'm surprised you heard the knock, it was a small tap so I wouldn't wake you just in case."

"I'm a mother. Small noises that might involve a kid trying to get my attention wake me up instantly."

"Right. Mom told me the same thing once." He pauses, clears his throat, and gestures toward the bed with a nod. "Mind if I sit?"

"Of course not."

Tossing aside the blankets, he takes a seat as I sit up and slip out of bed. "I'll be right back."

After using the bathroom, I wash my hands, brush my teeth, and attempt to remove all the tangles out of my hair because it looks as rough as I feel. Then, following a deep inhale and slow exhale to prep for the apology I know I have to make, I head back into the bedroom.

He looks up, smiling as I reenter the bedroom and pats the bed beside him. Once I'm seated next to him, he reaches over with no hesitation and clasps my hand in his, interlacing our fingers as he frowns.

Before he can speak, though, perhaps to say sorry for something he didn't even do wrong, I say it first because I'm the one who needs to. "I'm sorry."

"What for?" He angles his whole body so he's facing me completely, his deepening frown furrowing his brow and making it clear how hurt he is even if he won't admit it.

"You thought I knew all along. You didn't deceive me, not on purpose. I had no right to accuse you of anything like I did last night."

"Babe." He lifts his free hand and cups my cheek, a quick flash of his teeth as he smiles before his face grows serious again. "I might've taken advantage of the attraction between us, but I'd be lying if I said I hadn't hoped you would finally leave him because of it."

"Well, I left him as I should've a long time ago. However, I'll admit you were a bit of an extra push I didn't know I needed." It's hard to keep tears from gathering in my eyes. I feel like all I've done is cry for the past few weeks and I'm so sick of crying, but I know it's a good thing just like admitting my fears is as well. "I think him calling last night set me off, though. I might have left, but I haven't escaped. He lives here, has a life here just like me. Things could get ugly."

"They already were." He dips his head in with that truth, the one neither of us can and shouldn't ignore, and presses his lips briefly against mine as if in reassurance. "Let's stay positive and hope leaving was the hardest part."

"Me, too. I'm tired of fighting him."

"We'll fight him alongside you if he really wants one after finding out who is standing behind you." I feel his lips lift in a smile as he locks his gaze with mine. "Pretty sure I'd take him down in a fight."

With a small laugh at the picture that forms in my

mind, I move my hands to rest on his knees and say, "Thank you. Now, can we talk about something other than my asshole of a soon-to-be ex-husband?"

"That's a great idea since I came in here because I need to ask your opinion on something."

"I thought you came in here to check on me."

Now he chuckles, his other hand coming up to cup my other cheek, and after another soft kiss says, "That was the cover story. Your opinion is the true reason. Ready?"

"Sure. Go ahead. I just hope I'm able to advise to your satisfaction."

"Great. Now, imagine you're me and—"

"Impossible."

"And," he asserts in a slightly stern yet amused voice, "according to your brother, you're terrible at romance. He's not wrong, because you are terrible at romance, and you really want to tell this woman you've been dating that you love her." When I inhale sharply, he snickers and slides his right hand back to the nape of my neck, the pad of his thumb on his left caressing my cheek while he carries on as if he didn't just shock the hell out of me. "How would you tell her? During a hypothetical question, or would you wait until you could finally take her out on a proper date?"

It takes everything I have to even manage a whisper, his declaration shocking me even though it shouldn't. "Cole…"

"I know. I didn't want to wait any longer. I saw the look on your face last night and it killed me. I never want you to doubt how I feel about you, even if it means making a fool of myself."

So sweet my heart hurts. "Then my answer is, you should tell her again."

His relief is palpable as the slight tension in his hold disappears. "I love you, babe."

Responding to his words with any more of my own eludes me as the tears I've been holding back roll down my cheeks, but they are from pure joy at hearing those words from someone who means it, outside of my children.

Moving into him, lifting my arms to wrap around his neck and climbing into his lap, seems like the perfect thing to do. His left arm drops from my face to slip around my waist, and even though my instinctual reaction is to stiffen, I tell him through my sobs, "Don't let me go."

"I won't," he promises while keeping me secure in his embrace. "Not until you want me to."

It's a long time before I want him to.

LUNCHTIME ARRIVES BEFORE I finally head downstairs.

Cole left me roughly an hour ago so I could get a shower and change for the day, telling me he still has his other present to give me once I'm ready for it. But I figure that will have to wait until after I've eaten since I'm starving.

And when I enter the kitchen, the only person I find is Cole sitting at the center island peeling an orange, which surprises me.

Glancing around, he looks up at me with a grin as I ask, "Uh, where is everyone? Especially my children?"

"Dad's at work and mom has all the kids. She took them out for lunch at a place not too far from here."

I like how he makes sure I know my kids are close by and in good hands. "We're alone?"

"Yep." He points at the sandwich on the counter before pushing it toward me with one finger while setting his orange down on his plate. "After you eat, you'll get your gift."

Taking a seat directly across from him, I pick up the sandwich and laugh at seeing the huge layer of ham with two slices of cheese, shaking my head. "There's no way I can eat this whole thing. It's huge!"

He opens a drawer, pulls out a knife, and eases the sandwich from my hold before slicing it in half. Putting mine back on my plate, he holds the other in his hand and sets the knife down with a wink. "I was hoping you'd say that so I didn't have to get up to make another one."

"Sneaky."

"I believe you mean smart and efficient."

"Yes, that too."

He lifts both his brows, gives a silent and pointed look at my sandwich as he bites into his. Following suit, a companionable quiet falls between us until we're both done eating.

"There." I push the plate away from me. "All done. Happy now?"

He stands up, grabs both the plates and takes them to the sink, then washes his hands before turning to face me with one extended. "Yep, and getting happier by the second. Ready?"

The moment I step close and place my hand in his, he leads us out the kitchen door, locking it behind us before heading toward the garage. Thinking we're gonna go for a drive, I'm shocked when he stops right outside it, takes my hands in his, and lifts them while telling me to cover my eyes.

Doing what he asks results in a minute or two where I'm wondering if he's left me standing here like a fool because other than the sound of the garage door rising, I don't hear anything else.

Then, the sound of it lowering and Cole's hushed voice nearby once more. "Okay. You can look now."

Dropping my arms to find him standing between two bicycles is so unexpected all I'm able to do is blink for a second trying to understand what I'm seeing. Of course, he makes it easier by stepping forward with a laugh and holding out a dark purple helmet that matches one of the bike's frames.

Stupefied, I state the obvious while taking the helmet from his grasp, putting it on my head and securing it in place. "You got me a bike."

"Yes." He walks closer until our bodies are only a few inches apart and tips my chin up with his fingers, dipping in to kiss my lips softly before murmuring against them, "A new bike that's all yours, no matter what."

If I had any tears left, I'd cry for pure joy at this. "We're going for a ride? Now?"

"The next two hours are all ours. I figure we'll ride and head to my place, or spend the whole two hours biking. It's up to you."

The thought of being with him in his place where I know it will be easier to progress past kissing and cuddling causes every inch of me to run hot and cold at the same time. Remembering the way he brings my whole body to life with his touch and how much I miss it has me wanting to head straight there, but after Mason, the thought of doing anything sexual makes my heart pound as anxiety rises to the surface.

And like always he somehow reads my thoughts without me saying a word, searching my eyes as he cups my cheek in his hand. "Hey. No pressure. Anything we do is up to you, and I mean it. Going to my place? I believe we'll both feel better about even taking our shirts off if we're not in my parent's house."

"I'm not afraid."

He smiles and it's filled with love, understanding, and a little amusement because we both know I'm lying through my teeth. "Yes, you are, babe, but that's why you're gonna take your power back, one step at a time. And I'm going to do anything to help you, even if it means letting you tie me to a chair while you ride me."

With that I laugh, the visual of tying this virile,

strong man to a chair strangely appealing. "You'd like that wouldn't you?"

"We could find out together."

Swallowing hard in an attempt to control the jumble of emotions whirling wild inside me, I take a step back and nod toward the bike as his touch falls away. "Let's start with the bike."

"All right."

He puts his helmet on and walks over to his bicycle, hopping on as I do the same, and off we go.

In the end, the rain that starts to pour down out of nowhere as we reach town makes the decision about going to his place for me.

21

THE INSTANT we enter Cole's apartment, he pulls two towels out of the nearby cupboard, one of which he holds out to me as we both stand dripping on the wood floors in the entryway.

"Let's undress and dry off." He tugs his shirt over his head and drops it to the floor. "I'll toss everything into the dryer while we're here and get you something to put on in the meantime."

As my teeth start to chatter, I dart past him and into the bathroom, reaching in to turn on the shower as he leans in the doorway behind me. "I need to warm up."

Stripping out of my clothes, he watches me with hooded eyes and an unreadable expression, swiping up my wet clothing without a word as I step inside and shut the curtain.

I'm standing under the pounding stream of hot water with my hair piled in a bun on top of my head when he returns and joins me as part of me knew all along he would do. Moving close, our bodies are barely an inch apart as we stare at each other wordlessly, the steam whirling around us.

Dropping my eyes to his hands, I'm not surprised to find them clenched at his sides, and truly appreciate for the first time his self-control in not touching me without me having to even ask him for it.

He's bigger and stronger than Mason, but instead of feeling afraid as we stand here like I thought I would, all of me comes alive just like every other time we were this close while naked. Our bodies on the brink of touching everywhere, I feel his desire for me between us, and I want to touch him as much as I want him to put his hands all over me.

My heart and my body know the kindness of his touch and how much he loves me, and I desire nothing more than to feel that again with him right now.

Lifting a hand to touch his face, I run it down until it rests on his shoulder, and am bluntly honest with him because we'll both need it. He needs to know what's to come in this little interlude between us.

"I want you to hold me. Touch me everywhere. I might cry, but unless I say stop, don't stop."

He jerks his head back a little and shakes it. "Babe, I don't think…"

"It's what I want." Raising the other hand, I rest it on his other shoulder before placing my body flush against his and sliding my arms to wrap around his neck. "I want you, and I want to try because I know you love me."

He glances away, his voice hoarse when he looks back at me and asks, "I could make it worse. Touching you intimately could set you off and I don't want to hurt you—"

"You won't, and I promise I'll tell you to stop if it's too much for me." This time it's me pressing my lips to his, reassuring him with a soft kiss and a smile. "Hug me back, Cole."

His reluctance is notable in the achingly slow way he does as I ask, one hand gently placed palm down on each side of my waist, gliding along my slick skin until they meet in the middle of my back. He keeps his hands in place even when I suck in a sharp breath, our eyes locked together, and his forehead rests on mine as my body relaxes into his hold.

"It feels so fucking good to have you against me like this," he finally whispers. "But this may work better if you tell me where to put my hands next. No surprises for either of us."

Seeing his point and wanting to make this easier for both of us, I remove my arms from around his neck and say, "I'm warm now. Hot even. Let's… move somewhere more comfortable."

Not needing to be told twice, he drops his arms and steps out, letting me turn off the water and exit when I'm ready. Once we're both dried off, I take his hand and lead us out of the bathroom into his bedroom, only to halt at the edge of the bed with uncertainty.

Feeling the heat practically radiating from his body as he stands behind me, I step back against him while directing him as he requested. "Put your arms around me."

Slipping them around my waist, he chuckles and lowers his head until his mouth is close to my right ear. "Bossy Leighton is hot. What next?"

Letting my head fall back on his left shoulder, I cover both his hands with each of my own and guide one up my body while inching the other down. Finding it easier to keep relaxed when my own hands are touching his, I keep them overlaying his as one cups my breast, the other slipping between my legs after I part them and adjust my stance.

His cock is rock hard against my ass, and he groans when I grind into him, his breathing growing harsh and tickling where his mouth kisses down my neck. When his fingers slip between my labia and discover how wet I am, we both moan, and with a deep breath I let go of his hands. He instantly ceases all contact with me as I whirl around and take a few slow backward steps toward the bed.

"On the edge." Sitting down, I wait until he's standing between my legs before speaking again, my skin flushing with everything I'm about to say. "I want to watch you…and see your face. Just, um, don't lay on me."

Gathering what I want, he drops to his knees and after a nod from me gently grips my hips in his hands. "Okay. Anything else?"

"Yes." My eyes grow wet as I tear my gaze from his with shame I know I shouldn't feel but do. "I uh, the morning of Jenna's attempt, I went to the doctor to get tested. She rushed the results because I told her Mason cheated on me, and he didn't give me anything. I wanted to…to make sure…"

Unable to finish my sentence thanks to my throat clogging with emotion, his silence forcing me to look back at him, only to find him staring at me with nothing except love in his eyes. "I realize how hard it is for you to have to tell me that, and thank you. I would hate to miss out on my favorite thing to do because he's a cocksucker, but get that look off your face. You've nothing to feel guilty about, babe. It's all on him."

"I know…I really do."

"Good, because it's time to make you cry out for other reasons. Lean back." When I'm resting on my elbows while still able to see him, he smiles and says, "Ready?"

"Yes."

Instantly, his hands glide from my hips down my legs, modifying their position so my feet rest on his shoulders, and his hands return to cradle my ass. Well, one does; the other slips between my legs and joins his mouth in a slow tease.

Any ideas I had of watching him disappear as if they never were when Cole does what he's always done so well. Easing my upper body down onto the bed, my hands skim down my body until his hair is tangled in my hands, and my eyes slam shut as he licks me in the perfect spot.

Everything is great as his thumb circles my clit, all

the sensations and emotions I enjoy when he's touching me flowing everywhere, and my orgasm building hard and fast. Only it screeches to an abrupt halt when he goes to insert a finger inside me, my body tensing up almost painfully, and he pauses instantly while I release my hold on his hair and scramble back up on my elbows.

He opens his eyes and draws his head away to find me gazing at him. That's when I feel the wetness on my cheeks, the tears dripping down on my chest even though I'm so happy to see his face. He hasn't moved his hand from its position, but I can see he wants to stop in his face, and he's just waiting for me to say the word.

But I won't let Mason take this away from me, let him rob me of joy even while away from him, and force my words out through the tears. "Keep going." When he doesn't move, the tears fall harder. "If you don't want to, don't, I understand."

"I fucking hate seeing you cry, babe. That's all." He inches his finger deeper, waiting until my body tenses and relaxes before doing it again and again, keeping his eyes locked on mine the whole time until he can't go any further. Then with a stroke to send pleasure spiking through me he says, "I love you."

His thumb circles and strokes my clit on the outside, his other hand clenching my ass tighter when he inserts a second finger and slowly joins it with the other. As his touch begins to ease the fear and bring back the joy I had started to feel just minutes before, he grins at me and says, "You're the most beautiful woman I've seen in my life, Leighton."

Smiling through my tears, my emotions are all over the place as I whisper, "Thank you."

When his next stroke has my pussy clenching down on his fingers, he chuckles before leaning in, taking my clit into his mouth and sucking on it hard enough to tip me over the edge into the release I so desperately needed. His touch is gone instantly as I fall back onto the bed after crying out his name, but a second later he's gathering me in his arms and repositioning us to lay on the bed with his body cradling mine from behind.

I realize why when the orgasm subsides and my whole body is shaking with sobs. He's trying to comfort me, his arms wrapped around my waist to keep me close and kissing the side of my neck as he murmurs comforting words I can't make out through the sounds of my crying.

Him covering us both up as the cool of the room seeps in is the last thing I remember before long.

I'M ALONE in bed when I wake up and the door is cracked open a little, enough for me to catch the indistinct sounds of people talking. Realizing Cole is probably watching TV, I slip out of bed and head out the door, finding him sitting on the couch staring at the phone in his hand.

"Hey."

He sits up straighter at my greeting, leaning forward

to put his phone on the coffee table in front of him before looking at me and smiling. "You're awake."

"Unless I died in my sleep, yep, I'm awake."

Don't think he expected me to joke about it because his eyes widen for a sec and then he laughs, patting the seat beside him in invitation. "Just talked to mom. She's home with the kids and she said for us to take our time; they just started a movie."

"How long was I out?"

"About an hour." He watches me walk toward him, grinning when I stop in front of where he sits and leans back so his lap is open. "Take a seat. Any seat."

Choosing to straddle his naked lap, he simply regards me without saying a word as I wrap my arms around his neck and rest my head on his shoulder.

"We should probably head back soon," I mumble into the crook of his neck. "Much as I enjoy this…"

"You feel guilty for leaving Jenna and Dean with my mom." It's a statement, not a question, and my response is a nod as he sighs and encircles his arms around me to hold me closer. "To be fair, it was her idea, and they were all giggling in the background when I called. She said Jenna even seems to be enjoying herself."

"Good." I don't find it necessary to voice how much I wish she would be more of herself around me again because I already told him that in the hospital. "I guess a little more time with you won't make a difference."

"It won't. Plus, it's still raining like fucking mad outside." He turns his head toward my face and kisses my cheek before murmuring in my ear, "You all right?"

"Perfect."

"Yes, you come pretty close."

Lifting my head with a soft laugh to find him peering at me with such intensity, it's hard to imagine how I've lived my life so long without someone like him in it. "You're only saying that because you love me."

"And I love you because it's true."

"Are all men your age so open with their feelings?"

The corner of his mouth quirks up along with one brow. "I have no idea, but does it matter?"

"Probably not. It's just new to me."

"Will it make you feel better if I admit that makes two of us?"

Something in his voice makes me sit up straight so we're face to face, and his gaze drops to my mouth for a second before returning to my eyes. "What do you mean?"

"I've had girlfriends before. I've never told another woman I loved her, though."

The opening for a joke is too hard to resist even as my heart beats faster and harder than ever before. "So, you've told other men then?"

But this moment is even better when he plays along, his arms tugging to bring my body against his, and he chuckles while our breaths mingle from our closeness. "All the time."

"Should I be jealous?"

"Absolutely."

My whole body feels like it's quivering with all the emotions flowing through me as I prepare to open up my heart in a way I never thought would happen again. "Cole?"

As if he knows what's coming, he keeps one arm around my waist while the other skims up my back to the nape of my neck, resting there with a soft caress of his fingers as he kisses the corner of my mouth. "Babe."

With watery eyes, my arms tighten their hold around his neck as — for the first time in what feels like forever — I place my trust and love in the hands of another person with the delicate hope they won't crush it. "I love you too, and I have to admit it scares the shit out of me."

"You have every right to feel that way," he assures me with another light kiss, his eyes searching mine as he smiles softly. "And I'll make sure your love and trust in me are never misplaced."

"How do you always seem to know the right thing to say?"

"My parents have always been great role models when it comes to relationships, especially my mother. She's always told all of us that you never say anything unless you mean it, because what you say is likely to last forever in the mind of the person you've said it to whether you meant it or not. That means when I say something, I make sure it's the truth and never leave room for doubt."

As a tear slips down my cheek, he catches it with a brush of his lips, and the motion coupled with his love for me is so far removed from the first horrible night with Mason that I want to replace all the bad memories with good ones even if it will be harder than hell.

Whether he kisses me or I kiss him, it doesn't matter. What does is that the meeting of our lips reminds me of the one we shared on the Ferris wheel; passionate, sweet, and hungry for more. And when I finally ask him to make love to me, the feel of his arousal hard and hot between my legs making me want him beyond my apprehension, getting to that point isn't easy.

He positions himself near the entrance and drops his hands to his sides, letting me control our union in every way while his gaze continues to burn hotter than ever into mine. I see the knowledge of what this is in his eyes, and I know he understands; this is just as much a new beginning for me as it is a cleansing of a touch I want nothing more than to forget. Inch by inch, my hands clawing at Cole's shoulders as tears stream down my face, yet our focus is completely on one another.

Bit by bit, his hands find their way back to touch, skim, and tease my skin once he's deep inside me, making sure every part of my body and his feel nothing except pure enjoyment.

And after we've both found release in each other, the sight of his red eyes through my own blurry ones means that when he wraps his arms around me and I sink into his embrace, I'm comforting him as much as he is me.

22

"YOU'RE GOING to have to talk to me at some point, Jenna."

It's Monday morning, Dean's at school, and now I'm driving Jenna home after her two doctor appointments. She's been excused from school until after New Year's, and I'm hoping by then the mystery about who she slept with will be solved.

She's remained silent with me, although the counselor said she cooperated once I left the room, and it hurts more than angers me that she won't speak to me. I'm quickly running out of patience, however, because now is not the time in our lives for her to lock me out; not when we need each other more than ever.

"I don't know why you won't speak to me, Jenna. It hurts that you're shutting me out like this. Is it because I yelled at you in the hospital? I was scared and didn't understand why you would do such a thing." She continues looking out the window, but I'm determined to get some reaction — any reaction — out of her. "You slept with someone, sweetie. Who was it? And why would you try to kill yourself to get his attention? Nobody is ever worth killing yourself over."

At that, she laughs with way too much disbelief for a teenager, turning her head toward me and snapping, "No, we just wait for them to kill us apparently."

Good thing we're at a stoplight because my head jerks to hers with a startled, "What?"

"You think I didn't know?" She screeches her words, slamming her hands down on the dashboard, tears streaming down her face as she spits her repressed anger at me. "It's one thing for dad to treat me like I'm stupid because he's an asshole and I know he doesn't love anybody else except himself. But you? I know my mom and you think I couldn't tell he hurt you? And you just… took it, and acted like everything was fine. I'm not dumb!"

"Jenna—"

"No!" She glares at me, her whole face crumpling in misery. "He came and got us from our friends' house that next morning, just like he always does because he ruins *everything*. He said you were sick and to let you sleep, then he left to go to the store for something, so I snuck into the room when I heard you crying. Only you were laying on your stomach, crying in your sleep, and the blankets weren't covering you. I *saw!*"

Speechless, I don't even get to react because a car blares its horn behind me, letting me know I need to go since the lights turned. It's only a few minutes to the house, but it feels like forever, especially since Jenna falls silent and turns back to stare out the window.

It doesn't last long though. When I pull into the Whitfield's driveway and shut off the car once parked, she opens her door with one hand and faces me once more.

Her words are as miserable as the look in her eyes. "I hated him, even more after the next time we came back from our friend's, I could tell something happened, but you didn't act like he hurt you. I didn't understand why you seemed so sad since you'd been so happy after meeting Mister Vaughn, until the night before I tried to kill myself. I heard you crying, and I... I stood outside the door and listened to dad say all this horrible stuff to you."

My hands cover my mouth in horror, stomach swirling with rising nausea, and recalling everything Mason said that my daughter should've never heard. "Oh, god."

"I knew you wouldn't leave him on your own, Mom." She uses her free hand to swipe at her face, the misery turning into anger once more as she turns toward the door. "I told the doctor it was 'cuz of *him*, but it wasn't. You think you saved me, but you didn't. I saved *you*, and I didn't care if I had to die to do it. Remember that the next time you want to treat me like I'm just some little kid."

As she jumps out and slams the door, I want to yell after her, but what actually happens is I grab the keys and follow her out of the car seconds before my breakfast—and self-loathing—make their way back up with a vengeance.

ONCE THE KIDS are in bed that evening, Cole—who pretty much told me except for work and sleeping he wanted to spend all the time he could with me, Jenna, and Dean—and his parents join me in the living room at my request.

Having to tell them what Mason's done and that Jenna knew makes me feel as sick as it did this morning, especially as their faces fill with disgust and anger equal to my own.

Only they're angry and disgusted at Mason, whereas I'm blaming myself for my daughter knowing about what her father did at all. She's gone right back to not talking to me after earlier, and I can't blame her. I had given up and I wasn't going to dare leave him. I wouldn't want to talk to me either if I were her.

"What angers me," Mister Whitfield finally says from where he sits next to Nell on the couch with his hands clenched at his sides, "is how your husband hasn't reacted at all to the divorce petition, other than his initial acknowledgment to me the other day."

He's referring to when Mason was served at work and how he had merely lifted the papers and smiled at his boss before leaving for the day, showing up to work this morning acting as if nothing were different in his life.

A move which is classic Mason and doesn't bode well.

It's hard to keep the quiver from my voice as I respond with a softly spoken, "He's biding his time."

Cole, sitting beside me with his arm around my shoulders, hugs me closer to his side. "Yes, I bet he is, and it may be best to lay low for a while."

"No. I've lived in fear long enough, and he's done enough damage to us as it is. The point of leaving him was so he's no longer in control my life."

"Leighton—"

Nell starts to say something in a persuasive tone, but I pull away from Cole and stand up with a shake of my head as I address the three of them. "There's no way for him to hurt me now, not with you all aware of the whole situation, so I refuse to be afraid of him. He has a month to counter the divorce papers, which I am sure he will do, but the only fight he's going to get out of me will be in the courtroom if it comes down to that. Otherwise, my children need me; they need to lead as normal a life as possible, and I refuse to let them down like I have been all these years ever again."

Pivoting, I don't wait to see if any of them have anything to say to that as I leave the room because it doesn't matter. Staying out of sight from Mason won't keep him from planning, and it won't keep me any safer, due to the exact reason I stated before to Cole: both of our lives are here and there's no chance we won't run into each other.

It's bound to happen and I'd rather face it head on

rather than pretending it won't. Not to mention, I won't hide or be afraid of facing anything anymore, such as my daughter.

So, after reaching the top of the steps, I suck in a deep breath and let it out slowly before walking toward Jenna's room and knocking on the door.

"What?"

I enter without responding after she calls out, and when she scowls at me from where she's lying on the bed, keeping myself from sighing with exasperation is difficult. Not even bothering to ask, I perch on the edge of the bed, prompting her to scoot away before crossing her arms over her chest and looking away.

Silence hangs between us for a few moments, and I let it, studying Jenna for the first time in what is probably a while. She's a spitting image of me, tall and lanky like me already even though she isn't done growing, and I wonder how I hadn't realized how much she looks like a grown woman already. Considering she's about to turn fourteen, the fact she could pass for an adult disturbs me beyond measure and makes it clear I've got so much to make up for.

Because she was right. While she isn't an adult, she's certainly not a little kid anymore, and treating her like one isn't going to get her to open up to me.

When I finally speak, it's to a teenager who loves her mother so much she'd risk her own life to try and save a life. "I'm sorry, Jenna."

Whatever she thought I would say, it obviously wasn't that, her head jerking toward me and her eyes wide.

Reaching over, I grab her hand, thinking I'll have to grip it to keep her from tugging it out of mine, but I don't. Instead, she gives mine a squeeze in return and lowers her head so her hair hides her face from view, the deep and shuddering breath she takes breaking my heart even more.

"I'm sorry," I say again, knowing I have to say all this to her even if it's difficult, because all these years living as we have been is going to end up tearing us apart otherwise. "You never should've had to make a decision like that to get my attention, or to get me to wake up and push through the fear. I pretended happiness with your father so long to keep the peace, it's all I let myself feel and see in others as well, even if it wasn't real or true."

"He's not a nice person," she says, whimpering as her eyes once again lift to meet mine. "He's never been much of a dad either."

"You're right, he hasn't, but without him I wouldn't have you, and that would be worse because you—and your brother, of course— mean the world to me."

The tears threatening to escape from her eyes finally do so at my words, trailing down her cheeks, and her whole face crumples. "You don't hate me for what I did?"

"Sweetie, I would *never* hate you for anything." Appalled she would think that's ever a possibility, I open my arms for her and wait in silence, smiling with relief when she moves into my embrace. "But promise me you won't do something like that ever again, Jenna, no matter what."

"I won't. I…it scared me."

"Me, too." Hoping this is the beginning of a better relationship between us, I decide to wait on asking her questions about the one she kept hidden from me, choosing instead to say, "Whenever you want to talk, I really need to know everything, sweetie. I won't push you to talk about what's been going on with you at school, though. I just want you to know I'm here for you."

"Okay," she whispers, not saying anything else as she remains wrapped in my arms.

And that's okay because I know it's a matter of time, just like everything else in our lives now.

23

WAITING for April to arrive for lunch is nerve-wracking, especially because she doesn't know anything that's gone on since her wedding, as I wanted to tell her everything in person.

It's funny watching her walk toward our booth, which I made sure was in a sparsely populated area for the privacy we'd need, with a confused expression. Her gaze zeroes in on me, not straying from my face even as she sits down and sets her purse off to the side.

"You're not wearing makeup, Leighton," she finally says with a smile, relaxing her posture as she sits back. "I almost didn't recognize you without it after all these years."

I know what she means. Every time I look in the mirror, my face fresh and free of the cosmetics that had become part of my mask over the years, it's weird and yet now serves as a continual source of empowerment.

To see the real me peering back is strange and still

not a reality I'm used to quite yet. No more hiding or pretending is hard to adjust to after so long.

Before I can respond, the waitress takes our drink order, and upon returning promptly with them, I let her know it'll be a bit before directing my gaze at April and finally dropping the big news.

"I've left Mason. But—" I hold up a hand as she opens her mouth to say something. "Let me get all this out before you say anything, okay?"

She nods, her expression solemn, and waits for me to begin.

When I do, she rapidly becomes the most difficult person I've had to tell this to, but I know it's because she honestly had no idea of what Mason did to me at all. Not to mention I've kept this such a huge secret from her all this time, and the slow devastation on her face is impossible to block out.

Her dismay grows more the closer I reach the end, and when I get to the part about Jenna's suicide attempt, tears are running down both of our faces. She slips out of her side and comes around to mine, sliding in before wrapping her arms around my upper body and hugging me tight.

"You should've told me," she chokes out through her tears. "I know why you didn't, but I wish you would have. There's nothing I wouldn't have done to help you leave a long time ago."

There's no point in telling her I wasn't ready to leave, let alone acknowledge the position I'd ended up in, because we both are aware of it, even if it's nothing said aloud. "I know."

"Where are you at now? And how can I help?"

"Well, as I said before, Cole told me his dad is Mason's boss. So, once I decided to leave, we ended up discussing it while at the hospital waiting on Jenna to wake up, which led to Cole telling me his parents insisted we come stay with them. Their attorney drew up divorce papers, and Mason was served the day after Thanksgiving. I haven't heard a word from him since."

"That's not a good sign." She draws back, picking up a napkin off the table to dab at her eyes. "He's got to know where you're at by now."

Swiping at my face, I take a deep breath before releasing it slowly. "He does, and I don't think he's taking it seriously at all. Probably believes I'll be back home soon."

"You won't. I can tell how much happier you are already, and that honestly makes me so happy for you." Grabbing her purse, she opens it and digs inside until she pulls out her phone. "I'm going to call work and take the rest of the day off."

"Great." When she holds the phone up to her ear, I take a sip of my water before teasing her. "It'll give me time to tell you all about how Cole expressed his love."

Her mouth drops open, replaced in an instant with a grin that matches my own smile, and she holds up a finger when someone answers on the other end of her call.

When she hangs up, for the first time since we began

having lunch like this, we spend hours together filling each other in on all the good and happy things happening in our lives.

Parting this time is better than ever before, because the weight I've been carrying around is lifted now that I've shared with her, and it won't be long until we hang out again. Any time, anywhere, without the interference or input of Mason.

Freedom from him is sweeter with every second that passes, but the part of me which awaits for the other shoe to drop finally gets exactly that later in the evening.

MASON ARRIVES OUT OF NOWHERE.

Having stopped at the store for a few minor items on the way to pick up Dean from school, my body shakes while my heartbeat races, every inch of me running cold from sheer fright at finding him standing by my car after exiting the shop.

The chance to turn around and head back inside without him catching sight of me is shot as his eyes fixate on me, almost as if he knew exactly when I would walk outside.

Even if I went back inside, something tells me he will either wait out here or follow me until I acknowledge him. There's no restraining order, nothing that says he can't approach or speak to me, and we can't avoid one another forever.

So, with a sigh, I head toward him at a leisurely pace

sure to piss him off, and stop almost ten feet from where he stands by the bumper.

I don't bother feigning even a modicum of nicety, choosing to glare at him while clutching the handles of the grocery bags tightly. "What the hell do you want, Mason?"

His face remains impassive, not even a glint of anger in his eyes or stance as he stands there with his hands slipped into his pockets. "To talk."

"I figured the divorce papers made it quite clear I want nothing to do with you, let alone desire to ever speak with you again."

He laughs as if I'm joking, shrugging his shoulder as he takes a step closer, and holds out a hand as if he wants nothing more than to help carry the bags. "You've had your fun, Leigh. It's time for you and the children to come home."

"I would ask if you're delusional, but there's no question your sanity and common sense are lacking if you think I'll ever return to a life with you."

At that, his eyes flash and his lips twist for a brief moment before his face is expressionless once again, leaving his mouth to spew forth his filth. "No need to be such a bitch, Leigh, especially when you're not an innocent victim. You think a judge is going to believe a jobless cheating whore without a home of her own is capable of raising two innocent children, one of whom has tried to commit suicide due to your failure to keep an eye on her while I worked constantly?"

Teeth clenched, I grit my teeth to keep from

responding in a way which will egg him on, but his triumphant grin at my silence ticks me off to the point staying silent is impossible.

"He'll believe it wiser than leaving Jenna and Dean in an environment that includes an abusive, cheating, narcissistic rapist and asshole, of that I'm positive."

"Really?" He chuckles, shaking his head and making a 'tsk-ing' sound, his whole stance relaxing into his usual no worries way. "I've got proof of you cheating on me, Leigh. What have you got, hm? The word of your lover and his father, my boss? Let me guess, you're fucking both of them now, aren't you?"

Disgusted, and wondering what kind of proof he thinks he has, the jibe back at him is easy and effortless. "Your mistake is believing me stupid enough not to make sure I have proof of the things you've done, Mason. Underestimating me for all these years. Shame on you."

The brief glimpse of uncertainty and alarm on his face would've been easily missed if I weren't intimately acquainted with every aspect of Mason and his moods. It's gone as quick as it appears, however, and when he strides toward me until the only thing blocking contact between our bodies is the bags, I don't flinch or step back out of sheer stubborn will.

"You don't have shit, Leigh," he hisses at me even as he pastes a polite smile on his face to fool anybody who might be watching. "Me, however? I knew all along and confirmed it quickly with some terrific photographic proof of you and him together. Outside and inside his place. Dressed one minute, naked the next, spreading your legs for someone from your daughter's school, and doing things with him you should only do with your husband."

Feeling the cover drain out of my face, I know he's not bluffing, and discovering he had me followed makes me sick with fear all over again. When he lifts a finger to caress my cheek, I shiver with revulsion and take a step back, which causes him to drop his hand with a purely nasty chuckle.

"That's right, Leigh," he says in a voice filled with triumph. "I told you what would happen if you tried to leave me, didn't I? Go ahead and hedge your bets, but you belong to me, and I'll always be one step ahead of you." Walking slowly backward, he tosses one final statement my way as if it's nothing more than a mere pleasantry before pivoting on his heel. "You've got two weeks, honey. Choose wisely."

Waiting, I watch him get into his car and drive away before woodenly walking toward mine, and get into the driver's side after placing the bags on the back seat.

Then, once I'm inside with the door closed and locked, all the pent up emotions rush forward, leaving me sobbing into my hands and knowing awful things are going to happen no matter what decision I make now.

I **MANAGE** to make it through the whole evening without anyone guessing something is bothering me. But the moment Cole and I are alone in my room before he heads home for the evening, I can't keep pretending any longer.

"I ran into Mason today." The statement is casual, as if it was no big deal while I pull my top over my head and toss it into the basket. "At the store before I went to pick up Dean."

"Did he say something to you?"

"Oh, yeah." Pushing my jeans down my legs, I smile at finding Cole scowling at me as I straighten, stepping out of my pants and kicking them to the side before walking over to stand in front of him in my bra and underwear. "He not only knows about us, Cole, but he also had me followed. He said he has pictures of us together… in compromising positions."

After studying my face for a moment, he lifts his hands to my face and cups my cheeks, then leans in and brings his mouth a brush away from mine before speaking. "Whatever you're thinking, babe, don't even go there. The worst he can do is share the photos and you get nothing in the divorce, which is what you've asked for anyway."

"No. The worst is he can use it against me in regard to everything *and* ruin your reputation."

"A risk I've been willing to take all along," he assures me as he draws away and holds my worried gaze with his loving eyes. "My job is not worth your life, Leighton, or the safety of your children. Dad will take me on if anything happens, so don't worry about me."

I hate the way his kindness makes me want to cry because I don't want the tears to spring up at all, even if the way he loves me fills me with such joy. Yet they do, leaving me to tell him everything even as tears trickle down my cheeks, the pain of knowing what's going to happen mixing with his gentle touch.

"He called me a cheating whore, said a judge wouldn't let the kids stay with me because I'm jobless and Jenna tried to kill herself. Accused me of sleeping with your father in addition to you—"

He touches his finger to my lips, stopping the stream of words with a radiant smile. "That's ridiculous. You're not my dad's type." I laugh at the absurd comment, which is exactly what he wanted, and he wipes the wetness off my cheeks before kissing me softly once more. "Focus on the good things, babe, and everything will work itself out."

"You can't know that."

"Just as you can't be sure it won't." He kisses me a final time, stepping back at the same time he drops his hands from my face, and says, "My family has friends in a lot of high places, babe. Let him say what he wants because his hands aren't clean by a long shot. But you have to stand your ground, because nothing we can do will matter if he gets to you, and you end up right where he wants you."

"It's hard to remember that when he's in my face, doing the same things he's always done. He knows what will send me into a panic."

"Of course." Slipping a hand into his pocket, he pulls out his phone and swipes the screen, tapping on it before putting it up to his ear while his eyes return to my face. "What was your degree in again?"

Blinking, it takes me a moment to realize what's he asking, and my face flushes when I answer. "English."

Both of his eyebrows rise even as he smiles, then holds up a finger when the person he called picks up.

"Hey, Mark. Leighton informed me that her husband approached her at the store today and threatened her, alleging he possesses photos of me and her together." He listens for a second, his grin widening at whatever the attorney handling my divorce is saying on the other end. "Did you? I would claim I'm shocked, but I'm not. Did we manage to get surveillance of him doing this as well?"

Another pause followed by a triumphant chuckle. "Idiot. Keep it on hand, in addition to everything else. Thanks, man."

Hanging up, he steps close once more and grabs my hand in his. "He's digging himself a grave, babe, and he's been doing it for a long time. All you have to do is hang in there."

The absolute glee on his face makes me want to ask what they've got on Mason, but I realize I don't care what it is, as long as it gets him out of my life as much as possible. And I don't want to talk about him anymore, not right now anyway. Throwing my arms around Cole's neck, I kiss the side of his neck while he wraps me in his embrace before asking, "Lay with me until I fall asleep?"

He doesn't answer, choosing instead to simply lift me and carry me over to the bed and climbing on with me in his arms as if I weigh nothing. Shifting to my right side, he curls his body behind mine, keeps his arm loosely around my middle, and skims kisses across my shoulder.

His whispered 'love you' is the last thing I recall before falling asleep, and when I wake up the next morning to him not being there next to me, knowing this is how it has to be for now doesn't make me wish any less that he never had to leave my side at night.

24

TWO WEEKS PASS without me running into Mason again, which is easily done when I don't leave the house unless I'm taking Dean to school or picking him up, or go out with Nell during the day.

The fact I spend the whole day waiting for something to happen, yet nothing does, makes me consider Cole had the right idea when suggesting Mason had hoped scaring me into submission might work best.

After all, it's been three weeks since they served him with the divorce papers, leaving him roughly a week to respond, and my lawyer says he hasn't been contacted by anyone representing Mason.

However, relief is far from what I feel, and it's due to understanding how Mason works. Give up? There's not a chance he will until he absolutely has to, and for that reason alone, my guard is now up at every moment.

And since today is the last day of school of the year, with the children having three weeks off for the

Christmas holidays, I'm heading up to the school to turn in the work Jenna's done at home.

Surprisingly, she asked to come with me, and since it's nearing the end of the day, I told her we'd go out anywhere she wants to dinner after picking her brother up; just the three of us.

Nobody—other than Cole and his family, of course—knows why Jenna's not in school, other than the general knowledge of her having a medical excuse. So, upon arrival, it figures the final bell has rung, and Jenna immediately catches sight of a friend she wishes to speak to.

The fact she turns to me instead of running off works in her favor as she asks, "Can I go say hi?"

"Sure. I'll be out in a few minutes after I give them your classwork and the release from the doctors to return to school."

"Okay." She smiles and starts to walk away before remembering her manners, tossing me a glance over her shoulder. "Thanks, Mom."

Turning toward the office door as she takes off, I head inside and the ladies at the desk are nice like always as they go through Jenna's classwork before moving on to the medical papers.

"How's Jenna feeling, Mrs. Wright?"

Withholding a wince at the last name I can't wait to rid myself of, I manage to offer her a tight smile. "She's better, thanks for asking."

"You tell her we're looking forward to her return,"

she says, handing me the papers back after copying them. "Hope you all have a Merry Christmas."

"Thank you. You, too."

The hallway is nearly empty when I step into it, and when I don't spot Jenna nearby, I head toward the noise coming from the gym thinking I'll run into her on the way. And I do, rounding the corner to discover her and Mister Graham standing right outside his room, having what looks to be a heated argument.

Halting, I take a step back to keep them from seeing me, peeking around the corner while trying to figure out what they could possibly be discussing. Noting it looks innocent after several minutes of what appears mere chatting, I'm about to stride forward when Jenna suddenly glares at him, whirling on her heel to stalk away only for Mister Graham to grab her upper arm to stop her from leaving.

It looks like someone grabbed her, babe. Hard.

He didn't mean it, just grabbed me when I tried to walk away…Just some asshole at school messing around, okay?

Cole's words from the phone call where he told me about the bruise on her arm, followed by Jenna's when I confronted her about it; her refusal to name the male she had sex with, the one who got her pregnant. All of it coming together in front of my eyes, but I don't want to believe it.

I *can't* believe he would take advantage of my daughter like that. Would he? Is this why she couldn't tell me? I don't want to accuse him without proof, because I know how damaging accusations such as those can take on a life of their own even if not true, but it's hard to deny what is right in front of me.

But one thing is for certain: if he is the one, I'm going to fucking kill him.

"Hey!" Yelling to announce myself, I storm toward them, pointing a finger at him when they both turn to look at me with equal surprise. "You take your hand off her right now!"

He removes his hand, holding up both with palms out as he steps back, and looks me straight in the face as Jenna wails, "Mom!"

Sparing a glance in her direction to find her gaping at me with a flushed face, I stop in front of Mister Graham, leaning in close to his face to hiss at him. "Was it you?"

"Mom—"

Tossing her a glare, she snaps her mouth shut while I refocus on her teacher, who now stares at me with confusion as he lowers his hands to his sides. "Was it me for what?"

"Putting your hands on my daughter in a way you shouldn't have, that's what."

His brows furrow more as he spares a glance at Jenna, then back at me with wide eyes, his face paling as his body stiffens when he gets what I'm implying. "Hell no. Why would you even think…what…?"

I don't know whether to trust if he's telling the truth or not, although he genuinely seems caught off guard by my assertion, and visibly relaxes as I put space between us.

"Mom," Jenna says again in a gentler tone with major attitude, stepping up next to me and putting her hand on my arm. "It wasn't him, I swear."

Continuing to keep my focus on him, my question is for clarification. "He didn't grab you just like that the last time?"

"No," she responds with a mumble, skin flushing all over again. "Can we leave now, please?"

"When I figure out what the hell is going on, sure." Pointing a finger at him, I ask, "Why did you grab her then?"

"I apologize, Mrs. Wright, I did it without thinking. I merely wondered whether she would be continuing her tutoring in the new year, or if you were going to get her an outside tutor again—"

Now that catches my attention. "A what?"

"An outside tutor," he repeats slowly. "She started to storm off when I brought it up, something which seems to be a habit of hers when asked something she doesn't wish to answer."

"Mom—"

"You." Turning to face her, I ignore the tears running down her face and release a humorless puff of laughter. "An outside tutor? You weren't even in tutoring after school as I thought you were, but with some boy! Who was it, Jenna? Your time to offer that information is over, this instant, and you will tell me right now."

Mister Graham clears his throat, offering up what I want to know in a soft voice as Jenna looks away in her refusal to tell me herself. "He's a Senior. Tucker

Andrews. They spent time together even on the days she skipped tutoring with me or left early. If it weren't for the note she presented me about the tutor, I would've contacted you…"

"A note?" Wow. This gets better by the second and as Jenna begins crying noisily at being caught, I nod at Mister Graham. "Thank you. And I apologize for assuming about—"

"Please." He holds up his hand and shakes his head. "Don't say it. I could see why you might get that impression, and I apologize once again."

The continued confusion in his voice makes it plain he's wondering why a simple grab would make me accuse him of something else entirely, but I'm not going to enlighten him. Schools are rumor mills, and the last thing we need the whole school to know about is that Jenna had been pregnant.

"Thanks for understanding." Snatching Jenna's hand with mine as it starts to drop off, I pull her along back toward the entry of the school, pissed off the whole way and making sure she knows it. "You're grounded. Way grounded, young lady. Forged note? Skipping tutoring and jeopardizing your entire future over some guy? For fuck's sake, Jenna, I don't even know what else to say!"

"I'm sorry!"

"I'm sure you are, and you'll remain that way for some time by the time I'm done with you. As for this boy, you'll give me his information and I'll be contacting his parents along with the police because he probably broke the law by sleeping with you."

When she makes a strangled sound, I don't even bother to look at her as we exit the building and head toward the car. Fury in my every step is punctuated with the slam of my door once inside, and no words spoken between me and her while I drive to pick up Dean.

Needless to say, we don't go out to dinner, and when we return back to the Whitfield's, she's once again hiding in her room while I'm left trying to come to terms as well as what to do with all the new information I've obtained today.

TUCKER ANDREWS TURNS out to be seventeen and, in conjunction with him still being a minor as well as the close in age exception law on the books, hadn't technically done anything wrong having sex with Jenna.

A harsh lesson for my daughter to learn when coupled with the fact the boy had used her, and she bore not only the emotional impact of her choices but the physical ones also.

But her lying and sneaking around isn't punished enough by merely being caught, and unfortunately for me, wanting to change Jenna's enrollment to an all-girls school for the upcoming semester requires Mason's permission since we share equal custody.

However, I wasn't going to approach him on my own, which is why I'm now sitting in a conference room with my lawyer, Mason and the lawyer he finally obtained on the other side of the table a mere three days after Christmas.

He answered the papers on the latest day possible, going all out by asking for full custody, which my attorney has assured me won't happen even if our divorce goes before a judge, as they prefer the parents maintain shared legal custody with one having residential.

I hate being in the same room, especially as he sits there being his usual manipulative self while trying to charm everyone in the room. If Mark hadn't pulled me aside before this meeting to discuss everything Mason's put his family through, and how revolted he'd been by the things I told him, I would be fooled right now into thinking he liked Mason.

But while his mouth is smiling, his eyes aren't, and I'm once again wondering what they've got on Mason that I'm unaware of. Whatever it is, they've assured me any threats he's made to me aren't likely to make it out of this room today.

"I want to settle this matter as quickly and painlessly as possible, I assure you." Mason ups his charm toward Mark, and when his lawyer hands over an envelope, mine only pulls them out enough to verify they're of me before setting them down. "As you can see, my wife carried on an affair with another man under the guise of going for a bike ride. Only her bike wasn't the only thing she rode."

"Mister Wright." Mark rebukes his comment with a sigh, the smile dropping from his face as he shakes his head. "There will be none of that here, please. Your wife wants a divorce and we're here to decide how best to make it happen, not exchange barbs."

"That will be difficult, as I don't believe she is a good role model for our children, nor the best person for them to reside with. She is a liar as well as a cheater and now lives with the family of the man she cheated with, who also happens to be my boss' son. Talk about a conflict of interest." He smirks at Mark and holds up a hand to prevent his lawyer from speaking. "Matter of fact, I don't believe you should be handling her divorce at all in that case."

"I figured you would say that."

Mark stands up and opens the door, allowing another man to enter before shutting it and reclaiming his seat while the other man takes over talking as if they've planned this all along. And when Mason starts to look panicked by this simple act, I finally see how the Whitfield's keeping an eye on things is going to work to my advantage.

"Now," Mark says while the other man remains silent, "Peter here will handle anything involving your divorce, and after he's done with that business, we will discuss your employment with Whitfield Enterprises."

"Pardon me?" Mason casts his lawyer a glance, and if I weren't afraid of Mason blowing up any second, I'd be amused by the look of bewilderment on the man's face. "What does my employment have to do with this?"

"We'll get to that, Mister Wright," Peter says, taking the information about the divorce from Mark and clearing his throat. "Your claims of adultery by your wife are valid. However, against advice from even her own legal counsel, Missus Wright has requested she receive nothing in the divorce. So I'm inclined to believe whatever your aim here, proving her adultery gains you nothing she's not already willing to give you to obtain her exit from this marriage."

"The children—" He starts to say, only to be interrupted with a wave of Peter's hand.

"Yes, yes, the children Mister Wright. Your daughter, her most recent trip to the hospital was the result of a suicide attempt, correct?"

"Yes."

"I have it on good authority you didn't visit your daughter in the hospital, Mister Wright. Why is that?"

Mason shoots a nasty look my way before answering. "I was watching my son. I didn't believe that sort of environment was good for him, so I kept him home with me."

"You didn't think your son would be worried about his sister, Mister Wright?" Mason has no reply to that, so Peter looks over at me and nods. "Perhaps you should fill in your husband on the situation with your daughter, Missus Wright, although I will do it for you if you wish."

"Thank you." Even though I know I should regard Mason with the same direct look he's giving me, years of self-preservation has me lowering my eyes as I speak to him. "You should be aware that not only was our daughter managing to have sex while at school, her suicide attempt also brought forth the fact she was pregnant by this boy, and—"

His mouth drops open, his triumphant look returning to his face as if he believes he's suddenly found the ticket to gaining custody. "Jenna's pregnant? On your watch, and you think you should have any custody of her?"

"Shut up, Mason," I snap, leaning forward and lifting my gaze to his in pure defiance, tired of him blaming me for everything. "She isn't pregnant any longer, and since she required immediate medical attention due to it, I had to make the choice because you weren't there. And again, it was happening at school, which is something I had *nothing* to do with."

"How can you believe you've nothing to do with our daughter being knocked up when you were fully responsible for her while I was at work?"

"Oh, I'm sorry, your parental responsibilities only exist when you're not at work? Silly me, I thought you were supposed to be a father at all times. Perhaps our daughter wouldn't have sought affection elsewhere if you didn't treat her like a pretty doll you can pull out to impress people, only to shove her aside otherwise."

"You left her at home with Dean while you went on your bike rides, and—"

Cutting him off, it's hard not to scream at him at this point. "I never left her alone with Dean when seeing Cole, even if I considered it a few times just to get the hell out of that fucking house. I only saw him on those rides when you were home, or when the kids were at their friends, so you can just stop talking bullshit right now."

"You're a whore—"

"Mister Wright," Mark begins but stops mid-sentence when I stand up and slam my hand down on the table.

"You brought your fucking mistresses to dinner," I shout at him, hating this man and myself for falling for him in the first place, lowering my voice as I continue in the face of his shocked expression. "So I hardly think you should be calling anyone names Mason. You just don't like that I did to you what you were doing to me, and you hate it, don't you? After all these years, controlling me failed and you can't take it!"

Turning to look at Mark after deciding Mason doesn't deserve to get away with his crap, I announce to them all, "I've changed my mind. I'm entitled to something after being married to this man for as long as I have been, and I will fight him for it if that's what it takes."

I watch both Mark and Peter's eyes light up with glee, which makes me confused for a moment until Peter opens the file and pulls out a thick pile of photos of his own, sliding them across the table to Mason's lawyer.

"You'll find these pictures date back years, time and date stamped, in which your client took various women on his business trips with him and engaged in overt public displays of affection with women who weren't his wife. In addition, he also used company funds for unintended and unauthorized purposes…"

I watch Mason's arrogance quickly deflate—and his fear rise—as the evidence of his wrongdoings not even I knew about before this moment stack in front of him, and I realize he's utterly screwed.

The Whitfield's had been watching him for years regarding his relationship with me, but also gained evidence of his embezzlement and fraud in the company the past six months to ensure a solid case against him. Looks like he's the one who hedged his bets and lost.

When I walk out of the building a little bit later, it is with the knowledge that not only would the divorce end up with me having full custody, but every single asset we have beyond the reparations required be made to the company will go to me and our children. Plus, witnessing Mason being arrested right in front of me is something I never imagined happening, but couldn't be more pleased about.

Of course, none of any of that will take away the pain of his treatment, nor will healing be easy or quick, because the damage he'd done not only to me but Jenna and Dean as well, will be something we all feel the effects of for a very long time.

However, I don't even try to keep the smile off my face as I head home to tell Cole and his family the good news, feeling as if the world's given me a belated Christmas present.

25

THE WHITFIELD'S decide to have a quiet New Year's at home, the decision spurred by the media coverage surrounding Mason's arrest involving their company, and feeling like a party just isn't a good idea this year.

With a half hour left until the ball drops, and the children laughing hysterically in the other room where the rest of the family is watching the festivities on TV, Nell turns to me as we're prepping snacks in the kitchen and suggests, "I can take it from here. In case you wish to get going, that is."

"Going?"

"Yes, with me!" Cole's declaration comes from the doorway before he strides over to me and wraps me in his arms with a grin. "I thought we could spend the night together. Alone."

"Did you?" It will be the first time we've spent the night together since the weekend at the hotel, and while the thought of waking up in his arms again is appealing, it's also a touch terrifying for various reasons. "Well, I'll consider it while ringing in the new year with my children, as I always do."

"Right," he says with an exaggerated sigh, winking to let me know he's teasing as he drops his arms and grins. "I knew you'd say that; the kids told me so."

Laughing, I lift up on tiptoe to give him a quick kiss before grabbing the tray of finger food that's ready to go and nodding toward the living room while holding it out to him. "Good. Now, please take this in there. We'll be there in a moment with the rest."

He mock salutes me before grabbing the tray and doing as I ask, Nell laughing the moment he's left the room. "He reminds me of his father so much at times. It's amazing how similar they are considering he died while Cole was so young."

This is the first time I've heard Nell mention Cole's father, so naturally I'm curious enough to use this moment to my advantage. "How similar?"

Her eyes grow misty as she looks at me, wiping her hands on a towel with a smile and a dreamy look on her face. "William was a good, faithful man and a hard worker. I fell in love with him because he was a beautiful person, and he never let me forget how much I meant to him. A romantic, through and through. I never had a chance of not giving my heart to him from the moment I met him."

I know that feeling, my heart squeezing for the love and pain in her words even as I joke, "Well, according to

Jack, Cole couldn't romance his way out of a wet paper bag."

She laughs, waggling a finger at me even as she continues talking, "His father was Cole's age when I gave birth. The moment his father held Cole in his arms, our son had his father wrapped around his finger, even though the notion of parenthood scared the crap out of him up until then. Whenever he wasn't working, he'd put him on his lap and read to him, and one evening I remarked on it, telling him it seemed like I never got to spend as much time with Cole like he did. He gave me the sweetest look as he took a seat next to me with our son in his arms and said, 'darling, we've got our whole lives, but I'll let you hold him this once,' before handing him over to me with a laugh."

I don't know what to say, taking a few steps closer to her before placing my hand over hers on top of the counter instead. "Oh, Nell. I can't even imagine…"

Her eyes flick toward the direction of the children's laughter, Cole's now added to it, before returning her gaze to mine with a curious expression. "I knew the moment my son fell in love with you, Leighton, because he came home with the same look in his eyes that his father had for me. And if there's something I've always known, it is that Cole is just like his father, and he has a loyal heart."

"I know."

"Do you? It's not that I don't like you, Leighton, because I do," she reassures me with a gentle smile when I frown, sighing as she slips her hand out from underneath mine and picks up the now finished tray of food. "I just wouldn't be much of a mother if I didn't have my fears, especially considering your situation, and I know you would feel the same way about your children.

I'm not trying to speak for my son, but he's always told me how much he wants a wife and a family, children of his own. He's not like other men his age and never has been, so all I'm asking is that you bring it up and talk about the potential future with him if you haven't already. And I say that because *both* of you deserve happiness, even if it isn't with each other in the end."

"I understand and I will." Nodding, I turn away to open the fridge as if I'm looking for something before glancing back at her. "I'll be in there in a few moments."

She aims another soft smile my way before walking out of the kitchen, leaving me to ponder what she said while trying to rid myself of the lump in my throat.

Because she's right. I would feel the same way about Jenna or Dean's hearts, and she's only put words to the thoughts I've had in the moments where I'm alone and let my doubts creep in.

I'm aware of how much Cole loves me. If it wasn't clear in his actions, him admitting I'm the only woman he's ever said the words to would've made it apparent he doesn't take our relationship lightly. And neither do I.

But children? I have two kids, and I'm not sure I want more. Becoming a wife again after my last experience with marriage? What if I never want to put myself in that position again? No, the two men don't compare in the slightest, but it's not about them, it's about doing what's best for me and my children.

One day, maybe; yet the question is, will Cole wait for one day? Much as it may not matter now, it might when it comes to having children of his own if he wants some.

After all, the last thing I want is to keep Cole from getting what he wants and needs.

"Are you okay, babe?"

Jumping at the sound of his voice intruding on my thoughts, I shut the door to the fridge before turning around slowly and asking, "I'm fine. I was just… looking for something to drink."

"Must've been some serious thought going into it, since I've been standing here for about two minutes now."

Feeling my face heat, I reopen the fridge and grab a water, then move toward him until we're nearly touching. Leaving the serious discussion for later, I grab his hand with mine. "Let's go ring in the new year and get the kids to bed, then we can go."

It's the right thing to say at this moment, and the only thing I want to say until we're alone since everything may change between us.

For now though, hope and love are the only emotions I wish to feel as I ring in the new year. And that's exactly what I get when he holds me in his embrace after kissing me at midnight while surrounded by both of our families.

To Break A Vow

TURNS out the last thing I want to do is ruin an evening alone with Cole, who spends his time making sure I'm relaxed and comfortable, easing us into making love by letting me control the pace once again before falling asleep wrapped around one another.

I'm feeling guilty about that this morning, though. We should've talked instead of me letting the selfish part of me—the piece of me wanting one last time to remember just in case—keep us from discussing something so important.

Now, after breakfast in bed, we sit side-by-side on the bed, his arm around my shoulders as he flips through the stations on the TV. Just as he sighs and turns it off after not finding something to watch, I manage to make myself blurt out, "We need to talk."

"Uh oh." Placing the remote on his nightstand, he angles his body toward mine and lifts a single brow, his tone teasing as he says, "Those are the single worst four words in the English language when strung together and aimed at a man from a woman."

"Cole…"

"What is it?" He instantly frowns, putting his hands on each side of my waist and lifting me, making sure I'm straddling his lap so we're face-to-face as he maintains his hold. "Tell me and I'll fix it because I hate when you're sad."

I laugh at that, even if it's a near to humorless chuckle, because wouldn't it be nice if he could just fix everything with a wave of his hand. Sure would make this easier, but since that's not gonna happen, I figure just forcing the words out is the way to go.

"Do you want children, Cole?"

His expression changes to surprised before he smiles. "Yes. I've always wanted to have kids of my own, eventually."

"I know, and you obviously love children. It's clear you'll make a great father."

"But…?"

His whole expression broadcasts the fact he knows what I'm about to say, which makes actually saying the words that much harder, but I make myself say it because we have to talk about this. "I…I'm not sure I want more children, Cole. Not to mention I'm already thirty-five and—"

"I don't give a shit about your age, Leighton," he cuts in with irritation. "I've accepted everything about you from the beginning, and your age isn't going to matter to me, ever."

"What about marriage? Do you imagine you'll want to get married someday?"

"Of course I do."

"What if I don't want to get married ever again? No marriage and no children for you by simply choosing to be with me."

He brings a hand up to his face, rubbing his forehead before sliding his hand down his face as if he can't believe we're discussing this before placing it back on my waist. "Where is this coming from, babe? Did I say or do something that's making you feel pressured about this stuff?"

"No, you didn't do anything." I won't tell him his mom said something to me. Not because I'm trying to hide it, but because I won't start trouble when his mother is just looking out for him by making me think about these things. "I've thought about it a lot in general."

"Why? I thought you realized all the what-if's in the world don't matter to me one bit."

"You shouldn't have to give up the things you want just because you love me, Cole, that's why."

"Bullshit. Isn't that what love involves? Making sacrifices?"

"No," I insist with a shake of my head. "Not if they are all one-sided."

"It's not one-sided. You feel how you feel, and I'm choosing to tell you I don't care. I won't live my life based on what-if's and might be's because neither of us knows anything about what might happen in the future."

"You should care." Climbing off his lap, I move to the edge of the bed, facing away from him as I try to get him to understand where I'm coming from. "Other than my children, I didn't get anything I wanted in my marriage, Cole. Even before we married, before the abuse started, I... I gave up so much for him. Do you think I wanted to merely be a housewife and a mother? When it became apparent that's what he wanted, after I fell in love with the part of him I didn't know was fake then, I told myself, well, it won't be forever. He agreed.

Just until we were done having children, and then I can do what I wanted to do all along. I didn't even consider it would end up any other way."

"That's not fair to me, babe." I feel him move on the bed, placing his hands on my shoulders while placing a leg on each side of my body, and sliding his hands down until he's embracing my waist from behind. "Just like you had then, I have a choice here, but unlike you, I'm walking into it knowing it may never change. Knowing you may always be my partner, but never my wife, and your children being the closest I'll ever come to having children of my own while loving them as if they *are* my own. And do you know why I'll do that?"

"No," I choke out through my tears, his arms tightening around me a little more as he presses a kiss on the back of my neck. "Why?"

"Because they are a piece of you, and I love you. Perhaps you see it as a sacrifice I shouldn't make because I may regret it, and other people might see it that way too, but I don't. I don't see myself losing in any way here. If anything, I'm gaining everything I've ever wanted, even if it's not how I pictured it would happen. But that's life, Leighton, and you have to embrace uncertainty even when you're scared shitless because you're just going from living in one cage with Mason to a self-imposed one otherwise."

Leaning forward until he removes his hands, I stand up and turn around to face him, whispering, "Promise me."

"Promise you what?"

"That if you change your mind, if it ends up not being enough, you'll tell me and not pretend like everything's fine when it isn't."

He raises his hands to my face and wipes away the tears on my cheeks. "As long as you promise me the same."

"I do."

"Then I do, too."

With that, he grins and pulls me into his embrace once again, sealing our vows with a kiss that quickly turns into more, and neither of us finding it necessary to acknowledge the symbolism of what we've just done with anything other than our hearts.

26

JENNA STARES at her new school with distaste as we approach it, continuing to whine when I turn into the parking lot, and really upping her dramatics when I park in front of the main entryway.

She focuses on me, her blue eyes bright with tears, dressed in her crisp, new school uniform. When she opens her mouth, I expect her to make one last ditch effort to change my mind about forcing her into an all-girls school.

But she ends up surprising me when she says, "Mom, I'm sorry I messed up. I'm upset because I'm really gonna miss my friends, but I know it's my fault you're sending me here."

"I want to trust you mean that, Jenna, so what you need to do is focus on school and getting your grades back up. I'd like to take your word for it, that you get why I'm doing this, but you'll need to show me you're serious about your future."

She nods a few times, tears slipping down her cheeks as she grabs her book bag from the floor. "I know. I didn't like when you said you were disappointed in me because you always told me and Dean that it would be pretty hard for us to disappoint you, so I know I really screwed up."

Reaching across, I take her hand with mine and smile at her, a little guilt creeping in for making her so sad even though she needed to understand how wrong her actions were. "All you ever have to do is try your hardest, Jenna, and I will not be disappointed. You weren't doing your best before and you're going here because boys are the last thing you should be focused on after everything that's gone on."

"It was stupid."

"Well, you made some bad choices, but we both know I haven't made the best decisions myself. Doesn't mean we can't begin trying our best from now on."

She glances out the window, biting her lip as if in thought, and turns back to me while asking, "Does me not missing dad make me bad?"

Glad dropping Dean off at school comes first now so he doesn't hear her say that, I shake my head at her. "No, but make sure your brother isn't around when you want to say stuff like that or talk about him with me, all right? He doesn't know about everything unlike you and he doesn't need that in his head."

"Okay."

"Good. Ready to go in? They said you need to go to the office, and someone will show you around."

"I remember."

"You've got your phone?" She nods while grabbing the door handle and I remind her of one final thing. "Keep it off until after school, and have a good day sweetie."

"You too, Mom." After she gets out, she turns to shut the door, and pauses to ask, "Are you still going to the house to get some things?"

"Yep. Do you need something?"

"No. Just think nothing is worth ever going back to that house for."

"I understand, but I want all our photos and stuff. I won't be there long, I promise."

"Okay. Love you."

"Love you, too."

She shuts the door, slings her book bag over one shoulder while straightening both, and after one final glance back at me, heads inside.

And I drive toward the house I hope I'll never need to enter after today ever again.

FOLLOWING the third trip to put stuff in the trunk of my car, I take one final walk around the house to make sure I haven't missed anything.

Satisfied, I make my way toward the kitchen counter, snatching up my phone, only to see a notification about a missed call from Cole.

With a swipe at the screen, I hit the green phone

icon to call him back and freeze mid-dial at the sound of a gun being cocked behind me.

"You have impeccable timing, Leigh," Mason declares with a snicker, pressing the gun to the back of my skull while grabbing the phone from my hand and laughing hard. "Aw, you missed a call from your lover; no doubt to warn you of my release from jail not even an hour ago."

"How? You—" Licking my lips, I hope to keep him talking while I figure out how to escape him without getting harmed. "You were supposed to be held until trial because you're a flight risk."

"Released on my own recognizance, babe." He sneers the final word, chuckling again at my wince in response to his use of Cole's term of endearment. The sound of my phone shattering as it hits the floor barely registers due to him grasping my hair tight in his hand, pulling my head back as he whispers nastily in my ear. "Upstanding citizen alleged of committing white collar crimes. First-time offender. They didn't have a chance of holding me, merely persuaded the judge to at least take my passport, and that's really too bad for you isn't it?"

"Engaging in another crime isn't smart—"

"Shut up," he snarls, his teeth biting into the flesh of my ear until I cry out in pain before letting go. "You never learn, do you? You thought you won along with everyone else, but you're wrong, Leigh. I told you that you are mine, and mine only, forever."

Wanting to know what I'm up against, I let my demeanor change, submitting to his hold by forcing weakness and passivity into every inch of my body, as well as my words. "What are you going to do Mason? If I disappear, they'll know."

"Will they? Let's test that theory, shall we, since you're still stupid enough to misjudge what I'm capable of." He loosens his grip on my hair, adjusting his position until he's standing in front of me, blocking my body against the counter. "Now, we're going to walk out to your car, but first, put your wrists together in front of you with your arms against your chest."

Doing as he says, the first of my emotions betray me as he reaches into his pocket with his free hand and pulls out a zip-tie. Wrapping it around my wrists, he makes sure it's tight and a tear I'm unable to hold back slips down my cheek. It doesn't help that he holds the gun in one hand, causing fear of him discharging it right in front of my face to skyrocket and paralyzing me with anxiety at the same time.

He shrugs out of his thigh-length coat once he's done and wraps it around my body. Adjusting his grip on the gun enough he can continue holding it to taunt me, he zips up the coat to the point it hides the fact my arms are tied behind it.

"Don't want you to get cold," he says with a laugh before looping an arm around my waist and pokes the gun into my side. "Let's go, and don't forget to smile."

Smiling or not doesn't matter. Nobody is outside anyway; the neighborhood is quiet with everyone at work and the kids in school. Mason quickly shoves me into the passenger seat through the drivers door. Landing with my face on the seat, he's got the doors locked and grins at me when I finally manage to right myself in the seat.

Reaching into the pocket of the coat, he pulls out another zip-tie, and commands harshly, "Bring your feet this way, held together, and don't be fucking dumb enough to attempt to kick me."

Once I've done as he says, and he ties my ankles together before pushing my feet off the seat, he leans across the space between us to kiss my cheek. Then he starts the car with the keys I'd been dumb enough to leave in the ignition before my final trip inside the house, and drives away from the house whistling, one hand on the wheel while the other keeps the gun pointed directly at me.

As if I have a chance of escaping tied up like this.

I'd laugh if I weren't terrified I'm about to lose my life at the hands of a man who will never leave me alone as long as we're both breathing.

"WAKE UP." Something jabs me in the side, and I try to jerk away from it, only for it to stab me harder at the same time Mason's voice returns me to my real-life nightmare. "Fucking wake up, Leigh. You don't want to miss this, gorgeous."

Forcing my eyes to cooperate, the first thing I notice upon opening them is the fact I'm sitting buckled up in the drivers seat while still tied up and Mason's standing outside the car. He shuts the door, having left the window cracked the tiniest bit so he can talk to me I guess, and then points the gun that was in my side at me through the glass.

After a quick glance to examine my surroundings, it only takes me a moment to recognize he's driven us two hours north to a cabin we used to vacation at during the summer but haven't been to in years. Another car is parked not far from mine, the smoke billowing in the cold air from the tailpipe clueing me into the fact it's probably what Mason's using to escape and leaving me confused for a second as to what he's planning to do with me.

Dread quickly sets in though as I focus my gaze toward the windshield, seeing nothing more than the snow coming down hard and the expansive lake in front of my eyes that I know rests on the other side of the hill, and is no doubt completely frozen over.

I jerk my horrified gaze to Mason, words rushing forth as I plead for my life through my sobs. "Don't do this, Mason. Please, I'm sorry. We—we can work this out. You don't want to kill me!"

"That's where you're wrong." His eyes are as cold as the air surrounding us, nodding his head at the floorboard. "If I can't have you, nobody can, and the only way that'll happen is if you're dead. So, you're going to press the gas with your feet and not let go until you hit the lake. Or I can shoot you right now if you prefer. You've ten seconds to make your choice before I make it for you."

That's when I look down and notice both of my feet pressing against the brake pedal, where he must've put them before putting the car in drive. "Why are you giving me a choice?"

"I don't want to shoot you because I'd rather know you're suffering for the one to two minutes it takes for the car to fill up with water while you're unable to free yourself. Knowing you're freezing to death on top of drowning will merely be a bonus."

"Mason—"

"Three."

Remembering my purse is under the passenger seat with my craft scissors inside while acknowledging the fact it may do me no good, I decide to take my chances with the water. I can't even try to save my life if he shoots me in the head.

"Two."

Glaring at him, I move my feet from the brake to the gas, pressing it all the way down with my feet after shouting, "I fucking hate you!"

And then I scream as the car hurtles toward the icy lake, removing my feet from the gas pedal even though he told me not to because the slope of the hill does the job.

I only have seconds before the car will crash into the lake, and bracing myself as best I can in this position, I slam my eyes shut and keep yelling at the top of my lungs with the futile hope someone will hear me.

My hope dies a quick death as the impact jolts my whole body forward, the seatbelt being the only thing saving me from being tossed around the car before tossing me back at my seat. The airbag deploys inches from my face and for a moment I wonder if I shouldn't just let the cold and water take me.

It doesn't last long, though. The thought of leaving my children without me dries my tears and spurs me into action after a few seconds. Since the car floats at first, I take this time to begin wiggling my body.

Crunching my aching body forward toward the now deflated airbag, I move my hands inside the coat, bending my wrists outward even though it hurts, and lifting what little I can of my ass off the seat. Grabbing the fabric of the coat with my fingers, I pull it as hard as I can manage with my butt lifted, and nearly cheer when it starts to rise.

Panic begins to set in as the car finally starts to sink soon after, even though I know all I need to do is free my hands at the bottom of the coat in order to undo the seatbelt. I fear I won't make it, especially as the cold starts to seep in, but then I hear sirens.

They are so faint I'm unsure if they are close, yet intuitively I know it doesn't matter; if I don't free myself, I'm going to die in this freezing, watery grave.

The car is now engulfed under the lake's surface, the water rising and covering my feet while I work the fabric with my fingers. When my fingers peek out from the bottom of the coat, I let out a gleeful squeal. Twisting my body to the side, I skim my fingers along the hem at the same time and breathe a sigh of relief while using as much force as I can muster to press the seatbelt button.

When it pops free, I fall onto my side, using the upward motion of my arms to move the coat up and over my head until it's off me completely.

Shoving back the sobs begging to rush forth, I decide to skip trying to reach for my purse in case I can't get myself up again. Rolling to my back, I begin kicking the drivers side window with the heels Mason hadn't thought to take off my feet.

Over and over my heels connect with the window, pure desperation pushing me past the cold and exhaustion as the water reaches the bottom of the seat, until finally the glass breaks. Water rushes in, filling up the car faster. Knowing my hands and feet being tied will lessen my ability to swim against the gush, I force myself into a sitting position and wait as the water slowly rises to cover my body.

Just before it reaches my head, I breathe in deep until it hurts, holding my breath while closing my eyes and slipping beneath the water, only to open them once submerged.

Leaning forward, I use my elbows and knees to inch my body toward the opening. With a final silent prayer, I sit back on my heels before using them to propel myself through the window as the car continues sinking fast.

Kicking my feet, I shove my hands forward and down, not sure it will work but doing anything to keep moving even though I'm so tired. Swishing my head in the water from side to side, I locate the hole in the ice and focus on getting to the top before making my way in that direction.

However, it's farther away than it looks, and looking back at the vehicle's location generates pure terror in my heart because if I hadn't freed myself, I would be trapped in a seat belt and drowning right now.

The thought is enough to spark something inside of me to push harder, working my arms and legs as fast as I can to get my body to the surface, but it's not enough. Fatigue settles in along with the cold seeping into my bones. My eyes struggle to stay open while my heart beats slower and slower in my chest until finally I can't fight anymore or hold my breath any longer, my body desperately gasping for air it'll never find.

One of the last things I see before my heavy eyelids shut is the light of the sun through the hole in the ice disappearing, and the last thing I feel as water begins to fill my lungs and my body starts to sink back toward the bottom is a body wrapping itself around mine.

My final thought as the darkness takes over is how I hope my children know how much I loved them, and that I died trying to fight my way back to them.

epilogue

EIGHT MONTHS HAVE GONE by since my heart stopped for a few moments right as Cole rescued me from the freezing January lake in the nick of time.

Unbeknownst to me, the car given to me by his family had a tracking device installed on it — something the company apparently stuck on all the cars in case of theft or other incidences. And after I failed to respond to Cole's call, they'd quickly checked on the car's location to see where I might be going. They gave immediate chase as they realized the car headed away from town and alerted the police in the closest village by the lake as well when they realized where he was headed.

Mason's twenty-minute head start nearly proved fatal to my life as he wanted. However, his failure to leave immediately upon me hitting the gas sealed his fate, as they caught him trying to flee moments after my car slammed into the ice. Although it's remained unclear how he managed to have another car ready and waiting to escape with, the part of me that thinks he was planning to kill me long before that day is something I'll never be able to shove aside entirely.

After that, Mason pled not guilty to embezzlement, fraud, and attempted murder. Then, three months ago, he found a way to hang himself inside the jail cell where he awaited sentencing after being found guilty; instead of facing the consequences for his actions, he proved himself a coward in every sense of the word.

Although I didn't end up having to spend long in the hospital, I've spent every moment since dealing with occasional numbness along with loss of feeling in some spots, from the nerve damage in my hands and feet. Of course, the damage is the result of having my circulation restricted by the zip-ties and from the freezing temps of the water. The underside of my forearms and legs, along with my elbows and knees, are riddled with little slivers of scars from the glass cutting me while making my way to the car window.

The truth is, I'll probably never fully recover from the short time I spent fighting for my life.

However, I haven't let what Mason tried to do affect me because something great happened that day on the hill, and as the water tried to trap me inside the car. Not only had I made a choice to tell Mason how I truly felt about him, or chosen to take my chances in the water rather than letting him shoot me, I also fought through my terror and panic to free myself. I'd been determined not to let him win in a battle I never desired to be a part of in the first place.

I remained intent on returning to my children alive and in one piece and did my best to achieve it.

Now, I don't fear the unknown, because I know I'm strong, and that I can survive even when it doesn't seem like that's likely.

And the same thing goes for my children.

While Dean mourns the father he loved, never having seen the true evilness in him even though he feared his authority, Jenna doesn't mourn him at all. Witness as she was to the things he did, neither of us will ever be able to scrub from our minds no matter how much we wish the memories gone.

It won't stop me from trying, however, because we all deserve better. I won't let Mason taint the rest of our lives or rob us of the happiness we deserve by giving in to the fear he tried so hard to force on us.

Which is why Jenna and Dean's excitement at me asking if they'd like to go to the fair is truly wonderful. I don't waste a minute, enjoying every second I have with them, and we've become closer as a family because of it.

And each day we also smile more and feel sad a little less about everything that has occurred in the past year.

I'm hoping today's no exception as we get into the car and head toward the fair, one year to the day of when Cole and I walked head on into each other in that school hallway and all of our lives were altered forever.

Violet Haze

COLE STANDS by the Ferris wheel waiting for us.

He doesn't suspect a thing as Jenna and Dean insist they want to join us on the ride before scampering off to enjoy the day with their friends. Little does he know this ride's the only one we'll be taking because we have somewhere else we all need to go to.

They take the seat behind us, and once we're all in place, it moves to let other passengers on.

Interlacing his fingers with mine, his eyes crinkling at the corners when he grins at me, leaning in to kiss me before straightening as the kids giggle.

"What's so funny?" He asks loud enough to make sure they can hear him even though he doesn't turn around.

"Nothing," Jenna replies in a sing-song tone.

With both of them snickering again and likely to give me away, I squeeze his hand a bit and smile back at him as the ride continues to move, two positions away from the highest point where he kissed me last year. "Cole?"

"Leighton?"

"I have a question for you."

"Do you?" He lifts a brow, amused, and his expression switches to serious at my solemn nod. "Well, I'm sure I have an answer, and if not, I'm sure I can get a nice enough signal up here to search for it."

That sends Jenna and Dean into a fit of giggles once more, and with my own lips twitching with suppressed laughter, I say, "That won't be necessary. However, before I ask my question, the kids have one of their own first."

"All right."

Jenna shouts, "You have to look at us first!"

"Okay," Cole says as he angles his body toward mine and turns his head to look over his shoulder. "What do you want to—"

He cuts off mid-sentence, the rest of his question forgotten at the sight of Jenna and Dean each holding half of a banner, with one side saying, 'Will You' and the other completing the question with, "Marry Mom?"

Flicking his bemused gaze from them to me and back again, he clears his throat. "Well, you two, I'd marry your mother today if she wanted me to."

As the two of them squeal with excitement and I laugh at them, Cole winces while facing me again, the Ferris wheel finally delivering us to the top position in what seems like the perfect moment.

Tugging my hand from where it's gripped in his, I wrap my arms around his neck, aware the happiness in my smile is reflected in my eyes as I ask softly, "So, you'll still marry me then?"

His confusion at my question is both adorable and amusing. He stares into my face, his arms stealing around my waist and gripping the fabric of my shirt in his fists, and with one final peek at the kids, he asks in a rough and emotion-filled voice, "Are you serious?"

"Yes."

"I thought—"

He stops as I shake my head, studying this man who has become so important to me that I can't imagine him not being in me or my children's lives. A man who jumped into a frozen lake without thought in order to save me, breathed life back into me once back on shore, and hasn't left my side unless doing so is one-hundred percent necessary since that day; who sat beside me in court and supported me through my testimony during Mason's trial.

Not only does he take care of me in every way he can, he's also an incredible role model and father figure for Jenna and Dean. He's taking ballroom dancing classes with my daughter after she signed up and found out she needed a partner, while helping Dean improve his baseball skills whenever they have the opportunity.

My best friend and lover who, just last night, finally spent his first night in my bed while my children were under the same roof; that one being attached to the house we bought to begin building our life together. And also the man who woke up this morning, cooking us all breakfast before heading to the fair to help his sister-in-law with her booth just as he had the year before.

How could I not love and trust this man enough to want to marry him?

Even as tears fill my eyes, I manage to hold them back while responding to the question in his gaze. "I decided what I wanted from you wasn't enough for me after all. I've sacrificed enough in my life; I'm not willing to forgo everything we could have together because I'm scared and a little nervous at the ideas themselves, rather than marrying you specifically."

He tries to pull me closer to him, only to growl in frustration as the belt for the ride prevents that, and assures me, "I'm not in a rush, babe. Whenever you want to marry me will be the day you make me the happiest man in the world."

"We better hurry then," Jenna remarks with a dramatic sigh. "Now I know why I never ride the Ferris wheel. You two are gonna be late to your backyard wedding!"

Cole gazes at me with widened eyes at Jenna's (somewhat rehearsed) declaration, but before he can find his voice to say anything, I draw his head toward mine and cover his lips with my own. After a moment, he removes his hands from my waist to cradle my face and manages to keep the kiss sweet and clean while leaving no doubt about his passion for me.

As if I would question that at all.

"Yuck!"

At Dean's exclamation of disgust, Cole ends the kiss, drawing away the tiniest bit before murmuring, "I love you."

"I love you, too."

He drops his hands from my face as he asks, "Are we actually getting married today?"

"We will if you say yes," I answer with a teasing flutter of my eyelids as he clasps my hands with his again. "Are you saying yes?"

Instead of answering me directly, he turns his focus back toward Jenna and Dean as he says, "The answer is yes, I'll marry your mom."

I'm sure that right then, as the Ferris wheel finally

jerks into motion, the kids' cheers are being heard all the way back at the house by everyone waiting for us.

Then, as Cole puts his arm around my shoulder to draw me to his side, holding me close, I close my eyes to cherish this moment with every inch of my heart.

It's the perfect way to close the door on one part of my life while embracing the beginning of another, surrounded by the love and support of those who always believed in me and helped me believe in myself.

The future has never looked so beautiful or bright, and as we alight from the Ferris wheel to head home, I watch as Dean slips his hand into Cole's as if he's been doing it forever, and Jenna takes mine.

That's when I realize this marriage will merely be a formality because Cole's already family to each of us, and I'm overjoyed to make both our dreams come true even more.

However, the news involving the further expansion of our family will have to wait for after the ceremony when we're all alone, naked, and in the position that most likely resulted in said announcement being made.

A moment that will change everything once more and I know my future will be nothing like my past.

I can't wait.

THE END

Thanks so much for reading! I hope you enjoyed Leighton and Cole's love story! If you have the chance, please consider leaving a rating & review on the site you purchased this from.

Visit my website to join my reader's list!
I'll never spam you and, by joining today, you'll receive a **FREE** eBook!

AFTERWORD

Abuse isn't romantic.

Abuse is wrong.

Physical, verbal, emotional, or sexual, whatever form someone experiences abuse isn't justified in any way, shape, or form.

There's nothing sexy or loving about a partner who isolates you, talks to you as if you don't matter, makes decisions for you that you aren't a participant in, hits or chokes you to demonstrate their power and strength over you, has sex with you against your wishes, or engages in any form of activity which isn't **100% consensual.** In a relationship or not, if you let your partner know what they're doing is unacceptable, if you say no, if you fight back, *if they know you don't want something even if you are unable to say something and they don't care,* and they don't stop their actions immediately, it is **not** consensual.

Leaving abusive relationships can be dangerous, which is why if you're being mistreated, you should confide in a non-biased third party you trust if you have such an opportunity. Don't think nobody will listen, because somebody absolutely will, and don't be afraid of getting your partner in trouble for their treatment of you. If

Afterword

they were concerned about that, they wouldn't have put their hands on you in the first place.

And this doesn't just apply to romantic relationships either. Even if the abusive person is a family member, **you don't deserve it**, no matter what they say.

If you are in the USA and in any sort of abusive relationship and don't know where to turn, or **feel as if it's too dangerous to get away on your own**, call the National Domestic Violence Hotline at 1-800-799-7233 or visit their website at this link for more information.

Know that it is **your right** to leave your relationship, any relationship, at any time, if you choose to do so. Nobody, and I mean *nobody*, has the right to make you stay against your will.

And please, consider therapy. This book is just a story, a romance novel at that, and while I hope it gives hope to survivors of rape and abuse (as I'm a survivor of both myself), it's just that. A story. Stay hopeful, and most of all, take care of yourself first. Your safety is of the **utmost** importance beyond anything else. Things can be replaced. But you're one of a kind and irreplaceable. Don't let anyone make you believe otherwise.

<3 Violet

about the author

Hey! I'm Violet Haze. I am autistic & the mother of one cool kid. I've been writing and publishing romantic fiction since late 2013. The majority of my stories are steamy romance and *all* of them are stories of true love. Happy reading!

For information on other books you can read, including links to ALL the vendors, visit her website: www.authorviolethaze.com!

Want to contact Violet?
Email her at: violet@authorviolethaze.com
Search for "Author Violet Haze" on Instagram & Facebook!

www.ingramcontent.com/pod-product-compliance
Lightning Source LLC
LaVergne TN
LVHW041624060526
838200LV00040B/1418